Ivy Feckett is Looking for Love

Ivy Feckett is Looking for Love

A Birmingham Romance

———

Jay Spencer Green

Copyright © 2016 by Jay Spencer Green

The right of Jay Spencer Green to be identified as the Author of this Work has been asserted by him in accordance with the Copyright, Design, and Patents Act 1988.

All rights reserved. No part of this publication may be reproduced, stored in a retrieval system, or transmitted, in any form or by any means, without the prior written permission of the author, nor be otherwise circulated in any form of binding or cover other than that in which it is published and without a similar condition being imposed on the purchaser.

This book is a work of fiction, and any resemblance to real places, products, or persons, either living or dead, is purely coincidental.

ISBN: 1530417929
ISBN 13: 9781530417926

Also by Jay Spencer Green

Breakfast at Cannibal Joe's

"Savagely funny and deftly anarchic, Jay Spencer Green's writing is as exquisite as it is deliciously dangerous."
Lisa McInerney, author, *The Glorious Heresies*

"Witty, acerbic, and wired to words."
William Wall, author, *Hearing Voices, Seeing Things*

"Joe Chambers is a CIA operative working in Dublin. Assigned to an agency-fronted publishing house, his problems include, but are not limited to, errant MI6 agents, double-crosses, insane profit-making schemes, a Francoist dwarf and a tapeworm named Steve. He is an utterly reprehensible character, fond of submerging his head in a sinkfull of whiskey and fantasising about brutally murdering irritating teenagers. He is, in other words, the perfect guide to this bizarre and repulsive journey into Dublin's gutters.

Jay Spencer Green presents a twisted and exaggerated, but wholly recognisable vision of Dublin. A place of suicide bombings, mass canine culling in the Phoenix Park, 'cheap Moore Street socks (35 euros for 6 pairs)', online divorce and enough red tape and bureaucracy to drive a man to murder. A place where 'cat's cheese salad' and a dubious pork/human hybrid meat share the menu. It is a Dublin of no redemption."
The Bloomfield Review

"Bonkers. Weird. Surreal. Satirical. Politically incorrect. Clever. Absurd. Witty. Disgusting."
The TBR Pile

"A *Catcher in the Rye* for the Wi-Fi generation."
Carlton B. Morgan, novelist, cartoonist, musician

Available in paperback and eBook formats

For Mimi

Chapter One

For the name of that which is hidden reveals it not.
                                                    Exemptions 2:17

After a mere four hours and twenty-nine minutes of research in the library that day, Ivy Feckett had identified no fewer than 739 derogatory or euphemistic terms for the female genitalia. She might have located several more had she not then spent fifty-two minutes trying to decide how to order them.

She had eventually opted for simple familiarity, beginning with Twat, a perfectly repugnant word Ivy had heard being used only that morning, on the train, by a porky, prematurely bald bloke with postadolescent acne whom she'd taken for a certified accountant with two children and a small willy. He'd been bawling into his mobile phone while preening himself, boasting of his previous night's exploits. While no private investigator, Ivy had deduced that he wasn't talking to his wife.

Next came Gash, another revolting word, which not only sounded ugly but also conjured up ideas in Ivy's mind of battle scenes and industrial injuries. It was followed by a number of associated terms—Ivy had bracketed them together even though their origins were different: Wedge, Slit, Slash, Gorge, and Gnashville. The last of these, she reflected, at least had the virtue of originality.

As she read through the list to make sure she hadn't accidentally repeated any of the words, Ivy found herself alternately appalled and fascinated. One of the hazards of her new job, she had soon discovered, was regular exposure to humanity's inventiveness in producing forms of humiliation, ridicule, and outright cruelty, and this week's research was closer to home than usual.

Gnashville was followed by Spitehole, Spitehole by Goat Hole, Goat Hole by Nanny Crack, and Nanny Crack by Hellmouth. Then there was Fleshsplit and Empty Vent and Bone Zone and Scumcup. After that came Black Vacuum, Pig's Nostril, Bloody Hollow, and Bleeding Crypt.

Just horrible.

From a case study of English public schoolboy argot, found in a festschrift collection of papers by figurational sociologists, Ivy had learned how a single term from Cockney rhyming slang—Sir Anthony Blunt—had generated an entirely new set of allusions relating to cricket positions: Third Man, Midwicket, Silly Mid-off, Second Slip, and Snot Gully. They, in turn, had produced The Long Room, a reference to Lords' Cricket Ground, and that had resulted in Labiarinth.

Other terms pursued a more vulgar theme—Cumpit, Cumbag, Cum-de-sac, Cum Canyon—or made reference to geological formations that had 'inspired' their creators, such as Fingal's Cave, Wookie Hole, Blackgang Chine, and Mulch Gulch.

All told, 22 of these terms were derived from private educational establishments, 15 from institutions of incarceration, 19 from the military, and 10 from the stock exchange. The other 673 had been invented by misogynistic middle-class male novelists trying to reproduce the linguistic creativity of 'the street.'

There was Finger Mincer, Chopper Stopper, Goalmouth Scramble, Redskin Pass.

The Devil's Pocket, Satan's Sleeve, and Trucker's Hanky (as in the phrase, "It held as much spunk as a trucker's hanky").

The Ravine of No Return, the Dark Passage, the Temple of Doom, the Vicious End.

Meat Grinder, Slaughterbowl, Slop Bucket, Pink Pile-Up, Clapham Train Crash.

Sniffield Market, Billingsgate, Hong Kong Garden, Vulvahampton.

Tartspout, Red Snapper, Fleshpot Noodle, Skin Pan Alley.

Skinned Rabbit, Jugged Hare, Shrimp Dip, Elmer Fudd.

Ivy heard a voice.

Jenkin's Ear, Wounded Knee, Babi Yar, South Armagh.

"Vee?"

Split Mivvi, Bloody Peach, Manky Puzzle, Bearded Clam, and Fuck Mussel.

Red Oyster Cult, Gussy's Gluepot, Betty's Boucherie.

It was Sam's voice.

A slew of obscure terms she'd never encountered before: Skewy, Snart, Fush, Kout, Prewer.

Kadri, Couñago, Biffers, Spaves, Sprag.

Butterfinch. Spint.

And Mop.

"What's up, Vee? What is it?"

"What?"

Startled, Ivy raised her gaze from the page, marking with her pencil the sentence, "I'm ripping off those sopping knickers and coming for your slats," to see an expression on Sam's face that simultaneously communicated concern and bemusement. He scratched himself through his cheesecloth shirt as he spoke.

"Is there anything wrong? Yow've gone a particularly vicious shade of scarlet and yowr glasses are steaming up. Have yow let one rip or something?"

Emotions rushed Ivy from all sides, as if someone had started to pour scalding coffee down her throat but then thought better of it and decided to splash it into her lap, down her legs, and across her chest. She was able to distinguish, among these feelings, a guilt-tinged arousal caused by reading explicit porn, disgust with herself at finding such demeaning filth pleasurable, embarrassment at being discovered by Sam indulging herself in this way, and faint abhorrence combined with a sense of grievance at the suggestion that her change in pallor could be explained by shame at public farting, a sense of grievance in no way diminished by the fact that it had come from a man whose sweatiness she could taste, even though he was sitting on the other side of the desk, across an absorbent stack of encyclopaedias and thesauri.

With all the aggression she could muster, she whispered,

"NoSamIhaven'tdon'tbehorrible."

But he was unconvinced.

"Yow probably need to take a dump, Vee," he announced to everyone within earshot. "Y'know, Chairman Mao, he wouldn't let his ministers attend meetings with him if they hadn't had a dump first. He reckoned it cleared their minds."

This fascinating tidbit of information was, unsurprisingly, of no practical use whatsoever to the bespectacled widow two seats away researching pre-Famine Irish immigration to Erdington. Peering over her glasses, she admonished Sam in a soft Wicklow brogue.

"Shut the feck up. Some people are trying to work."

Never easily embarrassed, Sam merely leered back at her with his big brown eyes and wiped his runny nose, but Ivy had already scrambled to her feet and was collecting her papers together frantically. Since her complexion was fast approaching purple, she lowered her face so no one could see.

"Where are yow off to, Vee?" He rose from his seat as he realized she was leaving. "I haven't finished this chapter yet."

Ivy tried not to hyperventilate as she replied.

"I'm done for the day. I have to get back to the office to drop in the week's work."

"What about—?"

"—You can give me your stuff next week. It'll hold off till then."

He sat back down.

"Yow *are* still coming round tomorrow night, right?"

"Of course I am. Of course." She nervously pushed her specs back up her nose; she was already past his seat and heading for the library exit.

As she skittered through the desks and down the stairs, she took a series of deep breaths and tried to blot out what had just transpired. Fortunately for her, Nature was about to lend a hand. As she passed through the main doors of the library, she was greeted by a splendid, blinding glare, a bright summer's afternoon in June that had put both a frown and a smile on the faces of everyone in Centenary Square. The joy of surviving another working week had combined with an unanticipated warmth to overwhelm the usual melancholia that came with the territory, the territory being Birmingham city centre; while the frowns, caused by a perfectly understandable failure to pack sunglasses, *did* resemble the more traditional facial expression, they were mere simulacra, disguising a less traditional cheeriness.

Breezing through the square, Ivy resisted the temptation to pop into the Repertory Theatre to see what was on, distracting herself with thoughts of getting home and wondering, with an element of annoyance with herself, exactly why she'd asked Sam to help out with her research. The obvious answer, that he was quite brilliant, didn't satisfy her. Wasn't she brilliant enough herself? And it wasn't like she was helping *him* out, especially since he had his own research to do for his Ph.D.

Grudgingly, she owned up that she knew the answer. It was because she knew he wouldn't say no. She and Sam had grown up together. Of course, it was also because he was cheap, although he was cheap because he was a friend. A good friend. A friend who went way back. A friend willing to help another friend in need, regardless of his own commitments. A friend who was already getting on her tits.

She crossed over Paradise Circus towards Colmore Row and turned right, onto Temple Row West, changing to the other side of the road to avoid the Old Joint Stock pub and to cut the corner round the side of the cathedral. She pressed on with her head lowered because she could still feel the heat of her flushed face, not realizing that had she looked up, she would have seen many other Brummies equally pink; the sun's unusual heat rendered her embarrassment indistinguishable from their incipient sunburn.

Just past Needless Alley, she reached the doors of the Hartfield Foundation, the HQ of those very astute and discerning folk who had spotted Ivy's genius, who had hired her to produce a series of position papers on. On? On what, exactly? Even after a couple of months, Ivy still wasn't entirely sure. All she could infer from the topics she'd been asked to cover over the past few weeks was that it had something to do with human rights.

She took the lift to the eighth floor, stepped out into the pristine, faux-retro reception looking onto the cathedral gardens, and barely had time to prepare the counterfeit nonchalance of her "Hello" to a headset-wearing Jake, his limbs casually deployed behind the smoked glass reception desk, before Sylvia, their boss, flung herself from her office like a flamingo on fire, arms aflail. Ivy took a step back and almost found herself in the lift again, just as the doors were shutting. She was trapped.

"Ivy Feckett! You *really* have to get yourself a cell phone," Sylvia squawked. "I've had John Holt from the Vintners' Association on the phone all day trying to get hold of the woman who wants to bring back Prohibition."

Ivy assumed that this referred to her. Sylvia had stopped flapping, and Ivy realized that the flamingo effect had been caused by the shocking pink cowl-neck sweater Sylvia was wearing and her tight orange leather skirt.

"That wasn't what I said." Ivy was automatically defensive—it was her natural attitude, although Sylvia had been full of nothing but praise until today. "You—" But Sylvia cut her short with a dismissive wave of her hand, and the next thing Ivy knew, she was being escorted into Sylvia's office to prevent a scene from developing in the foyer. That couldn't be good.

"You saw what I wrote," Ivy continued, quietly, once Sylvia had reached the other side of her desk.

"How could I not, Ivy? It was in *The Guardian, The Times, The Telegraph.*"

"And *The Mirror.*" Ivy hadn't wanted to be seen as a snob, so she'd sent her letter to the tabloids, too.

"Indeed." Sylvia didn't seem impressed. "And do you think, Ivy, that one reason why your letter received so much coverage was the phrase 'During my ongoing research for the Hartfield Foundation'?"

Ivy shoulders fell. She didn't have much of an excuse.

"I'm sorry. I know I shouldn't have mentioned it. But I *really* wanted the letter to be published. And the case I made *did* relate to the research you assigned me last week: 'Forms of discrimination throughout history' and 'alcohol-related crime.' I merely put the two together to point out the negative role played by pubs in modern society."

As if by magic, a copy of that morning's *Guardian* appeared in Sylvia's hands, open at the letters page.

"You did, Ivy. To be specific, you said, 'Public houses, once valuable meeting places conducive to the maturation and expansion of the public sphere'—whatever that means—'and therefore of the well-being of our democracy, now function as conservative, segregationist, almost racist institutions, producing a form of soft apartheid'."

Sylvia looked up at her from the page. Ivy could sense that a response was required.

"I was only making the point that if we want our society to be integrated, then pubs will have to be more welcoming to people who don't drink alcohol. Muslims, for instance. Integration is a two-way street."

"This is incredibly irresponsible, Ivy. I couldn't care less about your argument. It doesn't matter whether I agree with it or not. What matters is that you abused your position as a contracted researcher with this organization to advance your own agenda. How am I going to be able to defend you in front of Mr. Hartfield when he comes in next week?"

Ivy gulped. Mr. Hartfield would be on the warpath.

"Mr. Hartfield is coming in?"

"Not Mr. Hartfield senior. Young Mr. Hartfield ... Ned. He will be taking over the running of things around here for a while—with my help, that is—for six months. I want you to come in first thing Monday morning, Ivy, so we can meet with him and sort this matter out. Okay?"

Ivy had little choice.

"Of course."

"We'll see what he has to say. Frankly, I don't imagine he'll be too pleased."

Ivy understood. She considered advancing further arguments but decided to save them for Mr. Hartfield. She could see that Sylvia was already tuning out.

And so she had. It was a Friday afternoon, after all, and Sylvia had no particular axe to grind with Ivy other than the use of the Foundation's name. Besides, she had lied about being on the phone with John Holt of the Vintners' Association all day: It had been poor old Jake who'd been forced to take the calls and deal with all the flak.

She pursed her lips and contemplated Ivy across the desk, brought her hands up to her mouth as though in prayer, and wondered if she'd paused long enough to torture Ivy sufficiently. She had.

"All right, Ivy. Off you go. Come in first thing Monday morning. Let's get this out of the way."

Chapter Two

Thy God is within thee and without thee and apart from thee and above thee and beneath thee and beside thee and cleaves to thee. Thy very spirit is thy God and not thy God, for how can that which is not of thy substance create thee?

Saint Theophobe's epistle to the Dalmatians 2:11

It was mainly to stop herself from thinking about the scolding she'd received at Sylvia's hands and the possibility that she might already be facing the bullet that Ivy indulged in sexual fantasies on the way home, a practice she preferred to consider more of an intellectual exercise than a form of kinkiness. Otherwise, she would have started to worry she was turning pervy.

The routine of travelling to and from the office every day presented her with free time she might have used more productively, but she had almost succeeded in convincing herself that using her imagination was a necessary antidote to the constant retrieval and analytical recording of dry facts. What really drove her, however, was that, against all expectation and intention, she had found within herself a deep vein of political incorrectness. And indulging it was, she confessed to no one but herself, great fun.

The journey home each evening was so mind-numbingly boring—even with her iPod cranking out Shonen Knife and Guided by Voices, in the vain hope of dredging up some last vestige of energy from the ponderous ocean of fatigue that seemed to hit her the moment she sat down on the train—that the only way Ivy could keep herself going was by attempting to picture the full range of possible sexual couplings between her fellow commuters on any given journey. Thus, she found herself that evening considering the insuperable challenges that would confront the weedy, weak-moustached, lank-haired 17-year-old student with the grey rucksack in the seat opposite as he probed to locate not just a position of comfort but one actually allowing for penetration of the rotund, muu muu–draped earth mother stood next to him on legs like alabaster pillars—hairy alabaster pillars—and as many folds of flesh beneath her breasts as under her chin.

Over her shoulder, Ivy had seen a sweet, petite, doe-eyed trainee beauty therapist enter the carriage with three friends of a similar young age and demographic. Who'd do for her? How about the unapologetic yuppie in the Armani suit with the wavy hair and nose like a shovel? No. Too obvious. Besides, what's a yuppie doing on public transport? He couldn't be the genuine item. Maybe a drama student. A method actor who couldn't afford to replicate the life of a real yuppie. No beautician for him.

The civil servant. He'd do. The starched collar, striped cotton tie, sensible socks. He looked a good ten years older than the beautician but they'd get round that if she kept her eyes closed. He'd want to look at her, mind, wouldn't he, him being a bloke and her being a beautician, and with him being a civil servant Ivy couldn't imagine him being any more adventurous than the missionary position. Would he balk at the tobacco on her breath, Ivy wondered, since it was universally accepted that all beauticians smoked. Beauticians and flight attendants. Known fact.

Commuting is not good for the human psyche, Ivy decided. It led to twisted attitudes towards one's fellow human beings.

The ten-minute walk home from Solihull Station was usually pleasant and unrushed, but even at 6.30 that evening it was roasting, and Ivy had to take off her specs on several occasions to wipe the sweat from her forehead onto the sleeve of her pullover. Yes, pullover. So it served her right. If she was going to insist on wearing a black woolly jumper in the height of summer, she was going to drip with sweat, unless she was willing to pair it with the shortest of miniskirts and no knickers, a combination she'd once seen in an issue of *InStyle* in a doctor's surgery. But Ivy didn't have a mini skirt, and she'd never dream of going out without any knickers on. In any case, she had the perfect skirt to match her sweater: The black woollen midi that her Aunt Kate bought her last Christmas. They went together perfectly.

By negotiating Streetsbrook Road, always busy, Ivy entered another world, the genteel, tranquil, eminently respectable realm of three- and four-bedroomed detached and semi-detached dwellings of Broad Oaks Road. Home. For the time being, at least. For this was a road of white, two-parent families with Mercs and Beemers and the odd speedboat or family cruiser in the driveway; Ivy's house, at the far end, was the exception. Not that there could be any such thing as the 'wrong side of the tracks' in Solihull. Ivy's home was as respectable as all the others, but also the only house on the street inhabited by tenants: Ivy, Maggie, and Siobhan. The landlord, Mr. Boyd—Ivy knew him only as Mr. Boyd—had a number of similar such properties in the immediate vicinity but chose to reside in Knowle, which was even posher than Solihull, if such a thing were possible.

As far as Ivy was aware, no one looked down on the girls for not owning their own home, even though Solihull could be rather sticky, and they generally got on extraordinarily well with the other residents, especially Mr. Naylor next door, who could be relied on to pop round and sort out any plumbing or electrical problems they might have, despite being a solicitor and, by his own admission, with no professional experience in either area (Mrs. Naylor could be a little distant at times, but Ivy figured that having to look after three children and entertain her husband's clients was bound to take its toll). There seemed to be a unanimous agreement to live and let live, to be courteous, considerate, and, above all, decorous in all circumstances involving communication between neighbours. All residents were permitted to get on with their lives, and everyone had a family and a life to be getting on with. In Ivy's case, she had Maggie and Siobhan to be getting on with.

The assault on her senses the moment she opened the front door brought a little yelp from Ivy that she hoped neither of the girls had heard. Maggie was berserking with the hair lacquer in front of the hallway mirror, like she was trying to mace the Invisible Man, and smoking a fag at the same time—she was a flight attendant, after all—so that Ivy's glasses were at once coated with a thick film and her nostrils filled with the pong of alcohol, Marlboro, solvents, and propellants.

"Hi, Vee!" Maggie welcomed her chirpily, the cigarette dangling from the corner of her mouth. "Bit roasty-toasty out there, isn't it?"

Ivy stifled a pathetic whimper of a sneeze and pulled a tissue from her laptop case. She nodded and sniffled, then double-checked her watch. It was only twenty to seven, yet Maggie and Siobhan seemed to be in an advanced state of readiness for the night ahead.

"Hot enough to burn the balls off a bulldog," she continued, as Siobhan swanned down the stairs.

"Hey, Vee. We're heading into town for a meal." Siobhan was wearing the same two-piece suit she'd worn a fortnight earlier for the polo match in Edgbaston. A twinge of jealousy at the sight of that long, flowing golden hair caused Ivy to sigh internally, the way she always did when Siobhan made an appearance. Her confident demeanour—slender but feisty—those sleepy eyes, and that small mischievous mouth. A cross between Drew Barrymore and Winona Ryder, Ivy always thought, only without the compulsive shoplifting or questionable taste in men.

Maggie interrupted her thoughts.

"There are four of us, from work. We're going into Brum … to DNA. See if we can't cop off with some fellas."

"Some poor unsuspecting eejit," Siobhan joked as she squeezed past Maggie and headed for the kitchen. "D'you want a beer, Vee?"

Ivy was preoccupied, using the same tissue she had wiped her nose with to clean her specs, but she was succeeding only in smearing lacquer over the oval lenses.

"No ... no thank you." Siobhan had already opened the fridge to retrieve a bottle of Stella, and when Ivy refused, she simply shrugged and took it for herself. Ivy was still the front-door side of Maggie but was too polite to squeeze past. She was prepared to wait until all grooming was done, and in the meantime attempted what she imagined was housemate conversation.

"I like your jeans, Maggie."

Maggie swung her hips in Ivy's direction and checked over her left shoulder to contemplate her own backside.

"Thanks, Vee."

She dipped her head to peer at Ivy through her jet-black fringe, then glanced down again meaningfully at her own backside and up again to meet Ivy's gaze.

"Juicy."

Ivy panicked. What on earth did *that* mean? Was it some quasi-cannibalistic homosexual bonding ritual she was being invited to participate in? If a girl tells you her bum is juicy, how are you meant to react? Is there a recognized code of behaviour for this sort of situation?

She flushed and managed to stammer out,

"Yes ... very tasty," thinking this would provide the right level of camaraderie without being either prudish or overly aggressive.

Maggie's eyes widened with momentary surprise and she feigned apoplexy.

"*I-vee!* You little flirt. I'll be keeping an eye on you." She rotated a little more so that Ivy could see more of her rear.

"Juicy Couture. That's the label. The brand name of my jeans."

Oh Jesus Christ, thank God for that, thought Ivy. She wasn't a lesbo magnet after all. Just culturally inept.

Maggie placed a hand, the one without the lacquer can, on Ivy's right shoulder as if to say, "You are a card, Ivy," and in return Ivy offered a wan smile and directed Maggie's attention to the doorway of the kitchen, where Siobhan stood with a second bottle of lager.

"Ta, love." Maggie approached Siobhan to claim the bottle, giving Ivy the briefest of windows to scamper into the front room to take off her boots.

She collapsed into the sofa, Mr. Boyd's cast-off sofa, to be specific, which always made Ivy feel a bit icky, an uncomfortable feeling when she was already grimy and slimy, so she pulled off her boots as quickly as she could and slid down onto the carpet. The volume on the hi-fi system, bought in the sale at the old Beatties store, was turned down low, unusual for a Friday night, and Ivy could just make out the strains of Emmylou Harris.

She was starting to wish she'd accepted that lager. She'd have to get up again if she wanted it.

It had gone quiet in the kitchen. Ivy figured Maggie and Siobhan were just swigging their beers and primping and prodding, but even with Emmylou down low, Ivy could sense something unnatural about the sudden change in atmosphere, and she had a feeling she knew what was coming. The dreaded Friday night invite.

Sure enough, after a minute or so, Maggie's head popped round the front-room door. She attempted a casual air so as not to make Ivy feel patronized or pitied.

"Vee. D'you fancy coming out with us? We could do with the extra support."

It was clearly a lie. Maggie, too, was "only gorgeous," as Siobhan was always saying. Those generous ruby lips and gleaming teeth and rich mahogany eyes. *That pair* didn't need support from anyone, let alone Ivy. It just made them feel better to ask her to come along.

Ivy looked up at her with a grateful smile.

"No thanks, Maggie. You're okay. I'm absolutely wrecked and there's vegetarian lasagne in the fridge. It's been a hard day."

"Are you sure?" There was no sign from Maggie that she was relieved at this response. They were both good like that, Ivy thought.

"No, honestly. But thanks for the offer. I think I'll just run myself a bath and have an early night."

It was plainly madness to be having a hot bath on a humid summer night, especially a Friday when she should be out in a park somewhere or walking by a river, but Ivy had decided it was necessary all the same. And necessarily the answer she had to give.

It was exceedingly tempting for Ivy to resent Maggie and Siobhan, to feel jealous of them or, even worse, to console herself delusionally that they were able to go out and behave the way they did because they were nothing more than a pair of superficial, shallow, uneducated flight attendants trapped in a vicious cycle of low self-esteem, self-hatred, and hedonism, whereas she was far more sensitive, brighter, and possessed of greater self-respect and dignity.

But that was plainly crap. Exactly the word Ivy said to herself, out loud, as she lay back in her excruciatingly hot bath and realized her wine glass was empty. She had succumbed to a large Sauvignon Blanc, which had made the long, tiring day a little more tolerable, and the bathroom window was slightly open so that a cooling breeze—what there was of it—could whisper along the walls, carrying the last chirps of the twilight chorus from outside as the day wound down. But now she'd have to get up out of the bath again to top up her glass, and she wasn't sure if she still had the strength to do it, especially with those tired, loose limbs. Crap crap crappity crap.

She shuffled herself up from her prone position, making waves that burned her shoulders as they washed over, and leaned forward for the glass, perched precariously between the taps. Come on, Ivy. You can do it. Think of the starving grape-pickers.

She did. She did. She did it. Anything for a cold white wine.

Still, crap. Plainly crap. Ivy was smart enough to understand that she was making a stab at self-justification rather than facing up to the facts. And the facts were that Maggie and Siobhan were genuinely good, decent, considerate young women and they liked Ivy and she liked them. They were always friendly towards her, always cheerful, always smiling. Never too serious about life. Jesus, Ivy thought, I would give my right arm to be able to go out with them on a night like this; have a few drinks, have a nice meal, meet a few guys, have a dance, maybe have a snog. But there was another fact that had to be faced up to.

And the fact was that Ivy was shy. Or, if we are really going to be honest about it, though Ivy hated admitting it, she was too inexperienced. She could never behave like Maggie and Siobhan because she was too scared. Too scared that if she went out with them, she'd make a complete fool of herself and then have to own up to being little more than a child.

That was what scared Ivy. Far better to feign disinterest, to present this façade of intellectualism. It saved her from the awful possibility of revealing just how inadequate, incapable, and naive she was when it came to men.

Yes, far better, she told herself, to stay in with a nice hot bath, a couple of glasses of wine, and one's own imagination. No one need ever know.

Chapter Three

Entered they the exotic house of Sing-gap-poor, but able were they not to tell man from woman.
The Song of Tanya 11:1

Nor was Ivy even remotely jealous when a half-naked man emerged from Maggie's room the next morning at half past ten, just as Ivy was about to descend the stairs to make breakfast. Possibly it was because she didn't have a chance to take it all in, to get a good look. She had turned her head upon hearing Maggie's door open and caught a glimpse of tousled fair hair, maybe the beginnings of a beard, and a pair of cotton boxers as the guest in question spotted Ivy and decided to make a dash for the loo without any thought of introduction. Fancifully, Ivy thought of Bjorn Borg; a young Bjorn Borg—though Maggie's guest was slightly heavier set—in his rugged, unshaven Viking days.

"Must be very scratchy," she said to herself.

Ivy had had no cause to be embarrassed herself, being already fully dressed. She liked to make the most of the weekend, and that meant being up and out as early as possible to get things done. Maggie and Siobhan often worked overnights or irregular shifts, so they rarely had a reliable routine to speak of. It was only by chance that the three of them were around the house at the same time this weekend. Ivy felt that it was largely down to her to sort out the mopping, sweeping, and hoovering, all of which she tried to do as rapidly as she could on a Saturday morning, to get it all out of the way.

She ate a quick breakfast—two slices of toast with margarine and Marmite—and drank a mug of strong tea before retrieving the broom, mop, and bucket from the utility room at the back of the kitchen and getting down to work.

It was never a chore to Ivy. She always regarded these unwanted, thankless tasks as opportunities missed by others for hours of reflection and introspection, for quiet and considered examination of the issues of the day—personal, political, philosophical, sometimes all three. She would turn on the CD player in the kitchen so that she had some classical music to accompany her cleaning and contemplation, and before she knew it she'd have the job done and a solution to whatever problem she'd posed.

She was three-quarters of the way through vacuuming the back room, having done the front room and the hallway, when she realized she was not alone. Out of the corner of one eye, as she turned from the curtains, she caught a movement by the door and nearly hit the ceiling in fright. The shriek she emitted was nearly drowned out by the noise of the vacuum, but it registered with Maggie, who winced at the high pitch and narrowed her eyes, which were barely open to begin with, little more than red, weeping slits either side of her nose.

Ivy's foot reached the vacuum's off button, and as the whirring stopped, so the tension seemed to fall from

Maggie's shoulders and the tension leave her jaw. Her hair, however, that immaculately coiffed and lacquered bob of the previous night, was still startled, stuck up hither and thither in spikes and splashes and spears, like a suicide of crows. Ivy couldn't recall seeing Maggie so pale before, and she didn't recognize the shirt, either. It looked like a man's.

"Vee … Vee … Can you give it a rest please, love? It's very early."

Protest would have looked like cruelty, and even as Ivy opened her mouth she saw Maggie wince again at the prospect of any sound at all, so she just nodded, and Maggie, realizing her message had been received and understood, turned slowly, delicately, to head back to bed. Ivy had never had a really bad hangover, not one of those head-throbbing, lager-red-wine-tequila-and-nicotine, precipice-of-puking hangovers, but she knew from the TV and movies that it was considered appropriate to be quiet around, rather than celebrate, those who had succeeded in achieving one, and she had no desire to persecute or penalize Maggie for the previous night's excesses, even if she'd once again managed to pull a total stranger in the process. It wasn't for Ivy to judge.

She packed away the vacuum and left the house for town, having decided that this was the best way to avoid antagonizing anyone and to give Maggie and Siobhan the necessary privacy to get to know their guests. The previous day's weather had carried over, so the walk into Solihull was a delight, regardless of the heavy traffic. Ivy was able to convince herself that, if she turned away from the road, the cars rushing by were the crashes of waves on the beach at Weston-super-Mare, the resort of choice for her parents when Ivy was a child, and now their place of retirement.

Her Saturday night trips to Sam's house could not accurately be called the highlight of Ivy's week, and she liked to affect that she went there only as a courtesy and because Nana, Sam's gran, had always been so good to her. Whenever Sam made reference at work to the previous weekend's visit or offered suggestions for the forthcoming one, she would do her best to feign indifference and sometimes even pretend that she might have another appointment that would prevent her from coming, despite her knowledge that it sent Sam into a mood. But since her mom and dad had bought the bungalow in Weston and she'd moved in with Maggie and Siobhan, whom she'd only known for … less than a year, it had to be … Sam and his gran and Sam's sister, Caroline, had become the nearest thing Ivy had to family in this neck of the woods, and it would have grieved her as much as it would Sam were she forced to miss her Saturday night stopover.

That particular Saturday, it was Caroline who opened the door to an Ivy laden with the Belgian chocolates and Australian Shiraz she'd bought that afternoon in Solihull. And once again, Ivy was reminded that she was forever condemned to be surrounded by women of preternatural beauty and virtue.

"Give me those, Vee," Caroline said, reaching out long, sinuous, muscular arms, her caramel-cocoa flesh set off by her tight-fitting white T-shirt. "You look knacked."

"Thanks, Caz." Even when Caroline was being candid, you thanked her. Nobody could be offended by her. Caroline was there to be worshipped, adored. Even heroin was addicted to Caroline.

And if you did take offence, what of it? Look at her, for God's sake. Six feet of pure Amazonian womanhood with a brown belt in Tae kwon do. Who would mess with that? Ivy watched her enviously as she carried the gifts through into the kitchen with one hand; those gifts she'd humped all the way from town were a mere trifle to Caroline.

It's fair to say Ivy wanted Caroline's body. Not like that, of course, though Ivy could understand why men stared at her. She wanted those long arms, those lithe, fit legs, that firm, taut backside, those broad shoulders, those green slate eyes. The differences between them, she knew, were as much to do with lifestyle choices as genetics—while Ivy spent hours on end sitting on her arse with her head lost in arcane texts about medieval invective, Caroline was down the gym or at the club practicing her patterns or lifting weights. No one could begrudge her that figure or those looks, given the effort that went into them. Ivy could be just as athletic, she was sure, if only she made the effort.

Yeah, right.

"Alright Vee?" said Sam as Ivy entered the MacPhersons' dining room. Saint Bernard's Road didn't quite have the same cachet as Broad Oaks Road, technically being Shirley and all, but Sam's gran's house was still a well-appointed three-bedroomed detached property, and one that still exhibited many of the indicators of bourgeois life, despite having Sam in residence.

He was looking up at her from the floor, where he'd already laid out one of the many board games that seemed to constitute the totality of MacPherson family in-house entertainment, notwithstanding the old Bakelite wireless on the mantelpiece.

"Come in, Ivy. It's lovely to see you."

On the far side of the room, in the dimmest corner, sat Nana, Sam's gran, Amanjeet. As Ivy's eyes adjusted to the gloom, she was able to see that Nana was sitting in her wicker peacock chair, a crocheted blanket resting loosely on her lap, her pepper-grey hair put up in a bun.

"Hello, Nana. How are you?" She stepped over Sam, who made no effort to get out of her way, and kissed his gran softly on the cheek.

"I'm extraordinarily chipper, thank you, sweetness. It's been positively Mediterranean this afternoon, don't you think?"

"Boilin'. Ahr," Sam interrupted impatiently, having arranged all the pieces on the board. "Think you can beat us for once at Swizzo! Vee?"

She'd been raised to always be polite when invited to someone's house, and she'd done her best to persist in this habit, but Sam's sarcasm, his challenge to her intellectual superiority, and his smugness in the face of incontrovertible evidence that he was jammy and deceitful and nothing else compelled Ivy to respond with undue haste, but before she could open her moth, Nana got in first.

"Ow! Lay off." From the comfort of her chair, she'd somehow managed to give Sam a swift kick in the small of the back.

"Don't be so rude then. Offer your guest a drink first. And at least be gentleman enough to take her coat."

Sam grumbled and rubbed his back before stirring himself. He forced himself up off the floor and motioned vaguely towards the kitchen, indicating that Ivy should lead the way.

"Coat!" said Sam's gran, stopping them both in their tracks.

Sam tutted. "Bttr gve me yr ct thn," he said.

Caroline had pre-empted Nana's offer of a drink and returned to the room just as Ivy and Sam were about to leave, thrusting a wine glass of what looked like flat beer into Ivy's hand.

"This one's rhubarb, Vee."

"Oh ... thanks."

"Not quite Shiraz, of course," said Nana, "but it's a good vintage. I've had it laid up for a couple of years. What it lacks in complexity, I think you'll find, it makes up for in aggression ... Cheers."

She noticed then that Nana had been nursing a goblet of the very same beverage. Not for long. She threw it back with undisguised relish.

"Ahhhhh! Good health."

"Bottoms up," said Sam.

Luck and deceitfulness, much to Ivy's chagrin, were two of the most prized qualities for participants in Swizzo! It was even advertised as "The unethical role-playing game of diplomacy, duplicity, and deception." And although Ivy loved playing board games and the MacPhersons had a house packed to the rafters with them—Free Will, Race to the Bottom, Transgressor, Torpid Turtles, and Poverty Trap, to name but a few of the better ones—she lacked the capacity for imputing dishonesty to others, which made her the perfect victim, gullible to a fault, when it came to games like Swizzo!, in which players were expected to strike deals with one another only to renege on them later in the face of other, more advantageous offers.

Although she was slight and frail and smaller than Ivy, Nana managed to give a strong impression of watching over the whole evening with an air of bemused detachment, even as she played along with everyone else, even as she became more and more tipsy, making increasingly outlandish promises to Ivy in her role as the secretary-general of the UN. Even as she lost and it became clear that she'd been stitched up by her own grandchildren, an eventuality she laughed at uncontrollably while the other three marvelled at her capacity to take betrayal and her own naivety in her stride.

After two and a half hours of fraught negotiations and rolling of dice and judicious use of trump cards, not to mention two more bottles of rhubarb wine, Caroline was declared the winner. Playing the CEO of a biotechnology firm, she had managed to secure patents to an entire range of new species then spread them across the globe with the unwitting help of Ivy, and eventually she had driven all naturally occurring species into extinction so that she effectively owned to the rights to all living things.

"God bless the profit motive," she cheered as Sam awarded her the title of Queen Swizzo. There was polite applause all round before Sam folded up the board and started to pack everything away.

"I can't believe you let her get away with that," he said to Ivy as she finished off her third glass of wine. A warm glow was spreading through her limbs, and she was still smiling despite Sam's reprimand.

"How could I say no to her?" she asked. "You offered no incentive for me to regulate international trade." Her words were getting slurry, but she could still put together a coherent argument.

"That's because I wasn't in a position to. It was Nana who represented the international labour courts, if you remember."

"Oh." Her head was fuzzier than she'd realized. "Who were you being, then?"

Sam looked rather sheepish.

"I was being Cliff Richard."

Ivy's face lit up. She pushed Sam playfully in the chest.

"That's right. I kept getting you confused with Richard Branson."

She giggled at her own stupidity.

"But of course!" said Nana. "*That's* why you kept singing 'Up, up and away in my beautiful balloon'—Sam, stop cracking your knuckles—It makes sense now." She bit her lip. "Because Cliff didn't sing that one, did he?"

Ivy shook her head gravely. Nana went on,

"It was some other nob."

Say what?! Ivy couldn't be sure. Was she completely pissed or did Nana just say 'nob'? Nana, who was easing herself up out of her chair gingerly, but smirking playfully, tried not to break into outright giggles lest the spell be broken and Ivy realize she was messing with her head. She had calculated aright that Ivy's faculties were on pause and that anything happening from that point on would be forgotten by the morning, and while Nana had never been a malicious individual, she could rival any banker for mischief after sufficient exposure to fortifying liquor.

"Take Ivy up to bed, Caroline, love. I think she's quite fatigued. Aren't you dear?"

Ivy looked vacantly at her glass.

"Night, night, Mrs … Nana," she said.

"Night, night, sweetheart," said Nana.

"Fatigued as a newt," agreed Sam.

Chapter Four

For who is it that carries you when you are on your back?

Orthaxis 6:4

In contrast to the vicious nightclub hangovers inexplicably pursued by Siobhan and Maggie every weekend, the hangover produced by Nana's rhubarb wine was a positive boon for imbibers. One particular blessing was its lack of any localized pain. No stabbing behind the eyeballs, no piercing, electric drill pressure at the temples, no pull on the cheekbones by insupportable flesh. Only a diffused weariness, an incomplete return to full consciousness. Victims sensed the world as though through a gauze curtain: images through Vaselined eyes, sounds through earmuffs. Suffering, if any, was dulled, delayed, unreal. What might, the previous evening, have been endured thanks to numbness could, the next day, be borne thanks to the very gradual resurfacing of the peripheral nervous system. The term "hangover" thus falls short in its denotation: This was a hangover that provided its own cushion. A wraparound cushion against the harsh, cold reality of post-alcoholic hypoglycaemia.

And for Ivy, clutching tightly to Sam, fists clenched inside mittens around his midriff, her head twisted awkwardly against his flat, bony shoulders, a rhubarb-wine hangover could not have been more welcome.

Every Sunday morning, this unlikely pair would kit up in Parkas, hiking boots, jeans—Ivy always wore jeans on Saturday night if she was stopping over—climb aboard Sam's 1960 Durköpp Diane TS-E scooter, and head out into the wilds of Warwickshire, or the even wilder Birmingham suburbs, in search of hidden treasure.

One Saturday morning at Earlswood Lakes two years before, Sam had been introduced by a fellow fisherman to the wonders of Global Positioning System units. He had shown Sam how to locate his precise position on the surface of the planet.

"You never get lost, and it gives the missus peace of mind if she doesn't see me for a day or two," he'd confided to Sam. This was a practicality that didn't concern Sam, but he'd always been a sucker for gadgets—calculators, Palm Pilots, Blackberries, he'd bought each one as it came onto the market—and after he'd spent a few evenings web surfing and discovered the world of geocaching, he had the perfect pretext for spending a couple of hundred quid on a Garmin eTrex Legend, justifying his selection on the basis of its additional memory and the accompanying software, although in truth his decision was made on the basis of the unit's translucent blue case, which matched his scooter perfectly.

For want of a more concise description, geocaching is treasure hunting for geeks. Geocachers hide boxes of goodies, called caches, at obscure locations around the planet and then post the co-ordinates online for other cachers to find. These boxes usually contain small, inexpensive items for exchange among cachers; small and inexpensive, but also something more. By their inclusion in the cache, these inconspicuous items convey very precise messages between people who need never meet, not unlike, say, Chinese fortune cookies or *Star Trek* Communicators. Indeed, a *Star Trek* Communicator would be just the sort of thing you might find in a cache. However, unlike the messages conveyed using *Star Trek* Communicators, which are usually warnings about hostile threats from Klingons or beaming up from an arid landscape, the messages conveyed by geocache items are principally benign and friendly. Messages of belonging. Messages that tell geocachers that they have finally found their tribe.

And that was part of the whole appeal for Sam. By engaging in this not-quite-solitary hobby, he became part of a community on his own terms, namely, in such a way that he didn't actually have to meet any other members of his in-group if he didn't want to. Not that cachers aren't a sociable lot once the ice is broken and trust is earned, but for someone like Sam, who sometimes found the company of strangers a trial beyond measure, a constant struggle to avoid looking awkward, to avoid *being* awkward, long-distance friends were often the best kind. Plus, it meant he didn't have to shower every day.

Ivy? Ivy, he dragged along having partially convinced her of the pleasure of the hunt, and Ivy had allowed herself to be swayed because there was little else for her to do on a Sunday morning but watch cartoons and try to stay out of Siobhan and Maggie's way as they disposed of the previous night's guests. Her mom and dad might have preferred her to spend the morning, unfashionably, by going to church, but Ivy was determined that if she was going to be unfashionable, it would be in her own way.

They'd left Caroline behind, practicing her Tae kwon do *tuls* in the front room—that was *her* Sunday-morning ritual—and headed in the direction of the airport. Through World's End, along the elegantly named Dove House Lane, along a Lode Lane busy even on a Sunday, past the Rover works, and onto the Coventry Road, Ivy refusing to relax her grip for a moment, aware that sustaining the tension in her body was crucial to confusing the rhubarb-wine hangover into hanging around. While she remained tense, she remained immune to the cold, to discomfort, and almost immune to the embarrassment of hanging onto the back of Sam as they tootled along on his self-styled "fartmobile."

"Round the back of the NEC, according to the map," Sam shouted into the wind so that Ivy knew how much further they had to go. She rubbed her helmet up and down against his back to acknowledge she understood. She daren't have opened her mouth for fear of swallowing air.

Sam took them off the main road in time for the NEC train station, down Bickenhill Lane, and brought the scooter to a halt just past a roundabout exit next to a trading estate. He wanted to check his GPS receiver to figure out how close they were to the cache.

"Not far, Vee. See?" He passed the unit back for her to have a gander.

"Looks like it's round the other side of the halls."

"Ahr. But I think there's a shortcut here. On the perimeter road."

She sniffled her assent, Sam put the unit back in his pocket, and they set off again around the back of the complex. The exhibition halls were deserted and the car parks empty, save for distant skateboarders bunched around a makeshift ramp constructed from display signs, planks, and inverted crates.

"Where the hell is everyone?" Ivy asked herself. Geocachers place great store in being the FTF, or First to Find, and usually as soon as a cache is published online and cachers are notified, there is a mad scramble to get to it first. Not today, it seemed. But then Ivy remembered that it was a chilly ten o'clock on a Sunday morning. All the normal people, all the muggles, were reading the *Mail on Sunday* in bed or taking their kids off to football or making love. Oh yeah. That's where they are, she thought. All the muggles are making love. And not just the muggles. All the other cachers too, no doubt, even if it's just with themselves. I'm on the back of a scooter riding around a parking lot in the middle of nowhere in the bloody cold looking for a box of Tolkien replicas and whiffle balls because I'm just *not normal*. Because Sam's *not normal*.

And who would want to make love to someone not normal?

Sam drove them through to the front of the NEC and turned left onto the Northway, heading away from the complex and towards the north car parks, before realizing that the cache had to be hidden somewhere in the plantations, the landscaped woodlands that marked the boundary. He pulled up in the northernmost car park and checked the receiver again.

"It's not far up there, Vee. In the trees. This looks straightforward enough to me. What d'yow reckon?"

"Do we know what it is that we're looking for precisely?"

Ivy tried to never sound bored. Simply asking questions, she had discovered, made it seem like she was interested.

"It's a medium-sized cache, I think. Shouldn't be too hard to find."

They left their helmets on the scooter and clambered up the grass bank into the trees. This was where the fun began—at least, that was the theory. The last hundred yards or so was always the challenge, and unless you'd been given clues by other, altruistic cachers, it was possible that this part of the search could take longer than the rest of the pursuit altogether.

It had been a cloudy morning, much cooler than the previous few days, but wandering among the trees Ivy could feel the warmth of the sun as the morning wore on and the hangover wore off. She was becoming irritable, and hungry, and the clothes she was wearing had started to itch along her inner thigh. She had begun scratching. Her forehead. Just above her ears. And although she'd had a quick shower that morning at Sam's gran's, she was beginning to feel grotty again.

She was leaning against a newly planted maple and rubbing her left cheek against her shoulder, wondering how much longer she could put up with this way of life, when an unironic shout of "Eureka!" wound its way through the woods. Relief and what passed in geocaching circles for excitement overcame her lethargy, and she pushed herself off from the tree in Sam's direction.

He had waited—considerately, he thought—until Ivy reached him before pulling a camouflaged Tupperware box from the undergrowth near a stand of birch trees. He had wanted her to be there for the opening.

"Shall I do the honours?" Ivy nodded and smiled, and Sam pulled back the lid to reveal ...

... to reveal the usual junk. A couple of figurines from an obscure fantasy game, a CD of "Teach Yourself Klingon," a model of He-Man, a plastic whistle, and a trilobite fossil. Sam pulled each one out and turned it over in his hands in exaggerated contemplation.

"Which one do yow think, Ivy?" he asked, but she already knew he was going to take the whistle. It appealed to the official in him: the referee, the stationmaster, the park keeper.

"Whichever you think. We could use the whistle to call for help. If the scooter broke down or something. Or if it gets foggy and we get separated."

He eyed her suspiciously. She was offering him an excuse for an option he'd already taken, although it was an excuse he didn't much care for. She was casting aspersions on his fartmobile.

Not that he could resist the whistle. They both knew that.

Cleverly, he offered Ivy the box from which to extract it, as though to suggest it had been her choice, and then flicked open the logbook. "We're not the First to Find," he mumbled, a little dejected. "Three others beat us to it. Must have got here in the middle of the night." But he signed his name anyway, with the pen provided, and then reached deep into his Parka, looking at Ivy but actually looking through her, concentrating on the search his hand was conducting of his inside pocket, and eventually pulled out a yellow-and-red-striped rubber centipede. This was Sam's calling card: He always left a centipede. It amused him to think of a newbie opening the cache and thinking it was real. That'd give them a fright, wouldn't it? One day, he'd like to be there when it happened.

He put it in the box and carefully replaced it in the undergrowth, in its original location.

"An excellent spot but not that difficult to find, eh, Vee?"

Ivy was secretly grateful for that.

"It's what always happens when a phenomenon becomes too popular," she observed. "It gets dumbed down. You lose some of the intellectual edge."

Sam weighed her words carefully before silently agreeing. He didn't for one minute imagine she was being sarcastic.

Chapter Five

Taking after them the shields of the Ephemeron, confused they the armies of Utensil. Yea, vexed thoroughly did they the captains of Nashua and the eggshells of Mendieta.

3 Johns 7:27

It was with some trepidation and not a little circumspection that Ivy went through her wardrobe the next morning to find the right outfit for meeting Ned Hartfield. While the prospect of their encounter didn't quite fill her with dread, it was traumatic enough for her to consider the right attitude to adopt: Contrite? Angry? Eager for debate?

Once again, she was struck by how few clothes she had. Maggie and Siobhan always seemed to be in different outfits, whereas Ivy had accidentally limited herself to a handful of skirts, a few pairs of jeans, five or six plain blouses, and an assortment of T-shirts she'd acquired over the previous decade. Other than that, she had one, dowdy, navy blue trouser suit and, by chance rather than choice, a pair of presentable high heels to go with them.

Well, that makes it easy, she said to herself. A trouser suit says, 'professional,' 'competent,' 'assertive'; these were three adjectives Ivy rarely applied to herself, but she figured that the best attitude to adopt was, if not a defiant front, something other than cowering deference. Who on earth did this Ned Hartfield character think he was anyway?

Fancy thinking he could swan in like this and treat his employees like serfs. Employees with more qualifications, of a higher intelligence, no doubt, and fully cognizant of their rights in the 21st-century job market. We'll just see who wears the trousers, she thought.

She lined up a playlist of soothing music on her iPod for the train journey into work: Albinoni, Bizet, Chopin. And instead of fantasizing about her fellow commuters, she ran through her notes for the week ahead.

There was a substantial amount of reading to be done, reading that would undoubtedly require a trip to the university library. Sylvia had suggested she use the Baykov Library at the European Resource Centre, where she could avail of a stack of material on Eastern Europe and the Soviet Union. She'd have to get the bus out there at some point.

It was a peculiar mix this week:

Forms of torture employed by the NKVD and KGB.
Forms of torture employed by the Spanish Inquisition.
Mortality rates from experiments carried out on humans in Nazi concentration camps.
Details of the various forms of execution sanctioned by the world's religions.
Drop distances for hanging.
Anglo-Norman torture implements.
Genealogy of the British royal family.
Statistics for lives lost in wartime during the 20th century in Europe and Asia.
Statistics for lives lost on building sites.

Statistics for lives lost in coal, diamond, and copper mines.
Statistics on AIDS deaths in Africa.
Details of profits made by pharmaceutical companies.
Crimes punishable by psychiatric treatment in totalitarian regimes.
Sins and their punishment.
Death squads funded by the CIA.
Graduates of the School of the Americas.

What a fun week it was going to be.

Jake's eyes widened with surprise at seeing Ivy in the office so early. He hadn't even had time to settle in behind the reception desk.

"Someone's very eager this morning," he said as he crossed the foyer from the kitchen and set down his latte. "You must be researching something exciting this week."

"I wish. Sylvia told me to come in to meet Mr. Hartfield." She lowered her voice to a whisper. "Is he here yet?"

Jake sat down and flicked his quiff in the direction of Sylvia's office.

"What do you think?"

It was only then that Ivy noticed a deep, throbbing hum vibrating the walls. Normally, she'd have assumed there were workmen using heavy machinery outside, but this noise, oddly, appeared to be emanating from Sylvia's office. A low, moaning drone, ponderous and menacing.

"What's that?"

"That's him." Jake's voice was reduced to a whisper.

Ivy furrowed her brow, confused. What kind of human being made a noise like that?

Suddenly, Sylvia's voice was on the intercom. Without warning Ivy, Jake had called through.

"Ivy Feckett's here to see you."

"That's great, Jake. Send her right in."

She felt a bit betrayed by that. She hadn't composed herself yet, and the peculiar noise from Sylvia's office had discombobulated her. She was about to come face to face with she knew not what, and Jake had deprived her of a chance to gird her loins.

"In you go, Ivy," Jake said matter-of-factly, as though unaware of Ivy's apprehension. "Can't keep the bosses waiting."

She approached Sylvia's door, took a deep breath, and gave a quick rap before stepping through. Do everything by the book, she told herself. Don't give them cause for complaint.

When she stepped through the door, the first thing she saw was Sylvia's back. The sun was shining directly at her through the window and was so low in the sky that, had Sylvia not been in its way, Ivy would have been forced to shield her eyes. Thus it was that, as Sylvia turned to greet her, the glare slowly lit the room, much as it would after an eclipse, and Ivy caught sight, for the first time, of Ned Hartfield, sitting in Sylvia's chair, smiling benignly, the sun roaring just above his head like a nimbus.

"Ivy," said Sylvia. "Lovely to see you."

What a big fat lie. Sylvia was clearly on her best behaviour, too.

"I want you to meet Mr. Hartfield. Mr. Hartfield, ..."

Ivy approached and he rose from the chair. And rose. And rose some more. He was six foot tall. Then six foot one, two, three, four. The man was an absolute giant.

"... allow me to introduce you to Ivy Feckett."

He reached across the desk—across the room, it seemed to Ivy—and extended a paw. No, not a paw. But a huge, thick, long, perfectly manicured hand.

"MISS FECKETT," he boomed—a posh, Silhillian accent—"I'VE HEARD SO MUCH ABOUT YOU."

Ivy felt the skin on her face peel back as the shockwave of his voice pulsed past her head. He hadn't actually spoken in capital letters, not even raised his voice, but the sound seemed to be unnaturally amplified from some cavernous chamber deep within the darkness of his powerful, toned torso.

At least, that was how she imagined it. The truth was that she'd been so stunned by the force of his voice that anything but first impressions were lost on Ivy. Ned Hartfield conveyed nothing but power, confidence, strength. He radiated positivity, from the vice-like grip of his handshake to that beaming, perfect grin he gave her as he reached towards her, a movement that he'd been told communicated a desire for friendship, a nonthreatening, generous gesture but which nine times out of ten scared the bejeezus out of anyone who met him.

It was only when she noticed that Sylvia had retreated to the door and that Ned was gesturing for her to take a seat, that Ivy was able to offer a formulaic reply. She sat down and said,

"All good, I hope."

Sylvia couldn't resist a parting shot.

"Mr. Hartfield and I have been discussing your letter to the papers."

"Oh," said Ivy. Sylvia gave a satisfied smirk and shut the door. Ivy found herself scrunching up her eyes and bracing for an onslaught. Here it was:

"Yes indeed. And I couldn't have agreed with you more, Miss Feckett."

Ivy wondered if her hearing had been damaged.

"I think you put forward a perfectly reasonable argument. Well thought out, intelligent, original, and cogent."

She hesitated before accepting the compliment. This had to be a ploy. A ruse. A con.

"Thank you, Mr. Hartfield. Thank you very much."

"Not at all. Call me Ned."

He leaned forward again, onto the desk, his fingers spread out, supporting him. For the first time Ivy relaxed and allowed herself to begin a more considered assessment of her new boss. Although the sun was directly behind him, forcing her to squint, she could see he was very young to be in charge.

"You're having trouble with the sun," he noticed. "Let me adjust the blinds." He went to the window, so that he was silhouetted in the sunlight. He raised one hand and a Venetian blind rattled down to the windowsill.

"Just turn that light on there, would you?" He indicated the switch by the door.

"Of course."

When she returned to her seat, he had resumed his previous position, like he, too, had rehearsed his lines.

"Now, what was I saying? Ah, yes. Your argument. I was very impressed, I have to say. You were quite right to point out the divisive nature of the alcohol industry as it is currently constituted in this country. You know, in Czarist Russia, the early feminist movement campaigned vigorously against the sale of vodka. Alcohol was so clearly implicated in violence against women and in the neglect of families. I was surprised you didn't bring that up as an example in your letter, to be honest."

She could see him properly now. He was *very* young looking. Skin so powder-pink that she wondered if his cheeks had ever seen a razor. Never needed one. So boyish. And yet not at all adolescent. Just a perfect complexion. Spotless. Creamy, even.

Cherubic was the word that eventually came to her. She had been only half-listening to Ned's speech, although the reference to feminism had registered. Yes, like a cherub, but with thick curly black hair that still seemed to reflect the sunshine when sunshine no longer penetrated the room.

And those eyes. Eyes of turquoise blue, as deep and clear as Caribbean waters. Ivy had been there as a young girl and returned with the belief that she'd never see that colour in

Nature again. Yet here it was, in those eyes gazing earnestly at her across the desk, searching her face inquisitively.

This was a man to fall in love with.

"A rower." With those shoulders, he had to be a rower.

"I'm sorry?"

Ivy jumped. Had she said that out aloud?

"Er … erm … Arrower. Edwina Arrower. That was the name of the author of the book on feminism in Czarist Russia."

"Ah."

He shook his head, his hair following gently.

"Doesn't ring a bell, but I'm happy to take your word for it. I'm impressed by your powers of recall, Miss Feckett."

"Call me Ivy." She got away with that one.

"Thank you … Ivy."

He sidled round the desk to sit on the corner nearest her. The scent of something spicy and woody and clean played around Ivy's nostrils. She tried not to inhale too obviously, but breathed in as she spoke.

"You know, I really didn't intend to cause any trouble."

"Trouble?"

"With the Vintners' Association. Sylvia said they had been calling to complain." Ned brushed away the thought.

"Oh, I wouldn't attach any importance to that. I know John—John Holt—we went to the same college at uni. He's duty bound to complain, of course, but these things have a way of working themselves out. A bit of to-and-fro, some feigned offence, some softening of attitudes, and before you know it, we have a new client. Just you wait and see."

Ivy wasn't entirely convinced, but his next words came as some encouragement.

"You know, Ivy, we really appreciate the work you're doing here for us. I realize you're only on a contract with us, and if that arrangement suits you, we're happy to accommodate you. But if, when it's over, you've enjoyed working here, I'd like to think we could make things ... shall we say ... a little more permanent."

At least, they would have been encouraging, but Ivy had been distracted by Ned's thighs. Thighs like tree trunks, the muscles visible through the straining fabric of his trousers. Incredible. Ivy was close to drooling. He was a rugby player. That was it. In the scrum. A hooker. A prop. A forward.

"A forward," she mouthed.

"Forward?" He repeated. She had done it again. "Am I being forward? I suppose I am. I do apologize, Ivy."

"No, no," she protested. "It's okay. I just meant ... You're very forward looking. It's a long way ahead ... the end of my contract."

He nodded and smiled.

"Ah yes, of course. I understand." He rose from the desk and held out his hand again. Ivy took this as her cue to leave.

"I have to be honest with you, Ivy. I've *so* wanted to meet you. This is such an unappetising job you have, in many respects, and when Sylvia described you to me, I thought to myself, 'I really must meet this resourceful young lady.' From Sylvia's description, I found it difficult to believe that

47

someone so … so … delicate could handle material of such an intense nature."

Ivy was still holding his hand. It was warm. She was warm. She was starting to blush again.

"Well, I hope I haven't disappointed you."

He squeezed.

"Good grief, Ivy, no. On the contrary. It's been a delight to make your acquaintance. You have surpassed my expectations. I hadn't anticipated that you'd be so …" He hesitated. For God's sake, thought Ivy, what's he going to say?

"So …"

He didn't look like he was searching for the right word. He had the word. He just hesitated to say it.

"Yes?"

He broke off, let go of her hand, and returned to the other side of the desk. Ivy stood there in shock. What had happened?

He rifled through the drawers in Sylvia's desk.

"Aha."

He came back round the desk and held something out to her.

"Would you mind if I ask you to use this, Ivy?"

"What is it?"

"It's a pager. I'm afraid it's a little outdated. It doesn't have a vibrate function … unfortunately … and it's very loud, but … and you can say no if you think I'm being invasive … but I'd like to be able to keep in touch with you during the day, if that's okay."

She took it from him and scrutinized its casing.

"Of course, of course. But if it's loud, I can't keep it switched on in the library. They won't allow it."

He slapped his forehead with the palm of his hand.

"I'm an idiot. I didn't think of that."

"Doesn't matter. I'll turn it on whenever I'm outside. You can reach me then. Does it have a memory function?"

"I'm not sure, to be honest."

"No matter. I'm happy to use it."

Ivy thought things were working out pretty well. He was promising to call her.

She stuffed the pager into her case and headed for the door. As she reached it, he said,

"Professional."

"I'm sorry?"

"I hadn't anticipated someone so professional."

She beamed.

"It's the glasses, I suppose. And the trouser suit," he explained. "It's very austere."

Was austerity a good thing?

"And I adore a woman in trousers."

Oh. Wow. It *was* good.

Chapter Six

The purest essence of herself offered she unto them, and most pleasing was it in the eyes of the Lord that they partook, lest it be wasted or they spit it out.
The Book of Snutt 1:18

She was useless for the rest of the day. Which is not to say that she didn't carry out the research she'd intended; she wanted more than ever to make sure she created a favourable impression. But whenever Sam tried to engage her in conversation or when she went to buy sandwiches from the deli round the corner from the library, she was incapable of meaningful conversation or rapid decision making. Her mind was miles away. Well, hundreds of yards away, back in the office where she assumed Ned was still sitting, with his beautiful, huge hands and his ridiculously impossible blue eyes.

And, for example, when Sam presented her with one of his moral conundrums, she couldn't string together two propositions, let alone formulate a coherent argument.

Sam and Ivy were forever contriving puzzles for one another, engaging in intellectual contests of no world-changing importance but immensely satisfying to them both. They felt their minds were being stimulated and that they were resolving issues yet to be dealt with by a society lacking their capacity for imagination and deliberation. They also secretly imagined that they were keeping their minds agile and developing their analytical and rhetorical skills for the inevitable day when they would be called on to exercise their talents for the good of humanity, never mind that their puzzles had become more like an exercise in flights of fancy, enjoying fantasies and daydreams under the cover of philosophical speculation. Entertainment value was as equally important as metaphysical or epistemological complexity.

"I read in the paper this morning," Sam began as they sat in the library cafeteria sipping cappuccinos, "of a case in the United States in which a baby had been born without a brain but which was being kept on a life-support machine."

"You mean it was brain dead, surely," Ivy said. Sam shook his head.

"Not according to the *New York Times*. The top half of the skull was non-existent. And no eyes or nose. Just a lower jaw, heart, limbs, other internal organs."

"And they managed to keep the heart beating and lungs functioning?"

"Apparently. At least, for a while. The baby died after a few weeks. Of natural causes."

"By death, I assume you mean the life-support system couldn't sustain it any longer."

"Indeed. Had it been taken off life support at any time, it would have died."

"And the definition of brain death couldn't technically apply."

"Quite."

Sam took a quick sip to let the scenario he had described sink in. Ivy had paid attention, but she was fidgeting. She was always fidgeting, of course; that was Ivy. Biting her nails. Chewing her hair. Agitation was her middle name.

"What this led me to thinking was: Assuming we can sustain the bodies of infants in this way—infants without brains and, therefore, with no sense of self and no possible chance of developing into a human being—what objection could there be to the mass production of embryos without brains in order to harvest their stem cells?"

"Huh. I see your point," said Ivy. But she didn't. Her mind had wandered off at 'therefore.' Although she'd given every impression of being interested, in reality she was trying to find the appropriate and precise adjective, the *mot juste,* to describe Ned's smell. By pinning it down, she reckoned, she'd be able to re-create it at will, without even having to inhale. And the re-creation of his scent would instantaneously return her to his office, Sylvia's office, and to the moment when he sat on the corner of the desk and she marvelled at his thighs. But the word just wouldn't come.

"It really is a problem."

"Isn't it? I'll leave it with yow, will I?" Sam was pleased that Ivy had failed to present an immediate riposte. "Let's for the sake of argument assume parental consent, though I'm not sure the term 'parental' necessarily applies to the production of nonsentient life forms … we don't generally refer to a bloke as being the father of his sperm or to a woman as the mother of her eggs, do we? That'd be a whole other argument. Can yow advance an objection—deontological or consequentialist, I don't mind—against the exploitation of embryonic stem cells under such conditions?"

Ivy was usually right on the ball, ready to cite a series of objections, resolutions, or counterintuitions, but this time she was happy to gaze into the distance, to give the impression of pondering some weighty issue. There was no way Sam could have known that the weighty issue that concerned her was how to conjure up the smell of another man's presence while ignoring him and his.

He finished his cappuccino.

"It looks like I've got yow stumped today, Vee. Working too hard if yow ask me."

Ivy broke off from her reverie.

"You're probably right, Sam. I am."

Daft is what I am, is what she really thought.

"And have you shagged him yet?" was Maggie's initial query that evening when she stumbled upon Ivy telling Siobhan about the new bloke in the office. Ivy had half-suspected it would be a mistake even to mention Ned to them, let alone ask for their advice on what to do.

"Well, no."

"She's pulling your leg, Vee," said Siobhan, a quick jerk of the head enough to convey her impatience, "Although from what you've told me, you already know more about him than Maggie usually does when she wakes up next to them the next morning."

"Heeeeey!" Maggie knew it was good-natured teasing—and rather an exaggeration—but it wasn't like she wanted the possibility openly suggested and broadcast. She exited the dining room, where Ivy and Siobhan had been conspiring and confiding, and made for the kitchen fridge and a glass of Chenin Blanc.

"I wouldn't know how to go about seducing him in any case," Ivy confessed. "Let alone what to do with him afterwards."

She was being unusually candid, for a change, but needs must; she hadn't entirely ruled out the possibility that she might, indeed, do something.

"Vee," Siobhan said, suddenly solicitous. "Do you mean to say you've never done it? Never shagged a bloke?"

Siobhan felt she was being allowed access to somewhere intimate, almost sacred.

"No, of course not. I mean, yes, yes I have done it ..." Siobhan didn't look convinced. "Of course I have."

It was true. She had. She was not at all the virgin everyone assumed. Not by any means. Blimey, it had been a whole nine years since she stopped being a virgin. After school, in the library, with Stuart Palmer. Now, *that* was one of the perils of unsupervised homework they never told you about: The danger of giggling fits following mutual embarrassment over joint perusal of a graphic biology textbook on reproduction and fertility among bonobos.

It had been a double dare between two naive, horny, sexually inquisitive teenagers, nothing more. And she hadn't even been all that inquisitive. It was a couple of months before she discovered that everyone else in her year knew him as Smeggy Palmer and she realized she'd been in a unique position to verify the rumoured source of that sobriquet. And she hadn't even had a peek. She remembered the soreness and the slobbering wetness of amateurish French kissing and the worry, yes, she remembered the worry afterwards, but that was about it. Oh yes, and the smell of Walker's cheese and onion crisps on his breath. That was sex for Ivy, thus far: Worry and cheese and onion crisps.

"What I mean is," she continued, "I doubt if I'll remember. It's been such a long time."

Siobhan gave her a comforting smile and a nudge.

"Don't fret, Vee. It's like riding a bike. You didn't fall off the last time, did you?"

Ivy shook her head.

"No, I didn't, but then I *was* firmly attached. There wasn't a saddle to sit on."

Chapter Seven

For the stomach of a cow is insufficient thereunto for the digesting of its food. The good Lord gave it four. And thy Lord hast endowed thee with two hands, that thou might hold both knife and fork.

Ahamster 11:12

Ned's head appeared around his office door.

"What are you doing for lunch?"

The question came out of the blue, so Ivy answered it honestly. There was no time to concoct a reply that might have sounded impressive.

"I'm going to the deli on Margaret Street for sandwiches. They give me a discount because I don't have relish."

He stepped into the reception area and fanned his fingers dismissively.

"Well, far be it from me to upset your routine, but how would you like to come with me for lunch? You won't have to pay for anything. We'll charge it to expenses."

Ivy had only popped into the office that morning to pick up a pass to the Baykov Library, and now she was being invited to lunch. Was this a date?

"Are you sure?"

"Absolutely. In fact, I insist." He took a step nearer and lowered his voice. "To be honest, Ivy, I could really do with your company. Sylvia's booked this God-awful pretentious place over by the law courts, and frankly I don't think I'd be able to put up with more than ten minutes in a place like that without some sort of escape route."

Not a date then. But not an invitation to pass up.

"What sort of food is it?"

"I'm not entirely sure. Probably some continental quiz-een." He enunciated the last word with a grimace that reminded her of Prince Charles, yet it seemed endearing on him.

"I'm willing to give it a try."

"Good girl."

He paused, realizing that such a condescending turn of phrase was regarded as offensive in some quarters.

"You will, I hope, be able to make some concession with regard to the partaking of intoxicating beverages."

"Excuse me?"

"I mean to say," his lips opened up in a disarming grin, "after our conversation yesterday, I wouldn't want you to think of me as a complete killjoy, a puritanical tyrant unable to show tolerance or flexibility."

"Nor I." Ivy was keen to play ball.

"That's good. You'll take a glass or two of wine with me, then. That's all I'm asking. And you mustn't concern yourself over any lost time. One afternoon of leisurely conversation won't do your work ethic any harm."

"Absolutely not. I'm working far too hard for you as it is." It surprised them both that she could joke with him like that. A nice surprise.

She hadn't dressed for a sophisticated, elegant afternoon's dining, but Ned wasn't the least bit concerned by that. His only concession to the restaurant's self-regard was to don a bright scarlet silk cravat in lieu of the tie that more conventional diners sported, in keeping with management's desire to maintain a certain 'tone.' Sylvia, for her part, seemed almost desperate to impress; Ivy was beginning to appreciate that although she was a mere contract worker, that status actually gave her an advantage over full-time staff on occasions such as these, especially someone like Sylvia, who was trying to build an entire career on the back of impressing her immediate superior at all times for the sake of a decent reference and another step up the think-tank hierarchy.

That desperation and eagerness to impress was also manifested in the choice of establishment. Chez Rabelais was the sort of place where the clientele went in order to feel bad about themselves. They knew they were going to be treated with contempt by the maître d' and the table staff, but they regarded such treatment as a guarantee of the restaurant's exclusivity and high standards. Not in a position to argue, the customers took it on trust that this was a high-class establishment. It had been reviewed as such in the national press—*The Observer Food Monthly,* no less—and although it had not yet secured even a single Michelin star, the *enfant terrible* chef had been profiled on local TV and had exhibited such hauteur that it must have seemed to viewers like he'd reached through the TV screen and given them the finger in the comfort of their own living room, a place of such hideous decor and taste that, ordinarily, he wouldn't have been seen dead there. To some viewers, it was the perfect provocation. They delighted in being scorned by genius. It was a sign of their own good taste to recognize genius, even if they had no standard by which to measure it other than the opinion of a journalist and the genius's own say-so.

"I can't decide," Sylvia said with typical submissiveness in the waiter's presence once they'd all sat down. "It all sounds so scrummy. Should I go with the sea urchin with seaweed juice or the squid stuffed with lemon, nuts, and the St. André onion?"

She looked across the table at Ned for assistance, at the same time trying to draw his attention to the utter sublimity and exquisiteness of the dishes, but when he shrugged with indifference, she swung round to Ivy and raised her eyebrows in exasperation. Ned was too polite to add his own exasperation, but Ivy suspected he was suppressing it.

"I'll have the haunch of rabbit," said Ned decisively to the waiter before telling Ivy from the side of his mouth, "It's the closest to normal food I can see among this rubbish."

Ivy gave a subdued, nervous laugh and tried not to play with her hair. She couldn't risk being so rude in front of Sylvia just yet.

"How about you, Ivy?" said Sylvia, placing the menu down on the table. She was looking for support. "Do you fancy the potted crab and pig's ear or the breast of albacore tuna with the velouté of root chervil and sorrel cream?"

"Tough call," said Ned. "Why not have them both?"

Ivy caught him looking at her from the corner of his eye and realized he was being sarcastic. She decided the risk was worth it.

"Actually, I fancied the shoulder of eel."

"Where?" said Sylvia, snatching the menu up off the table, but Ned had already spotted the joke and decided to play along.

"If not that, try the roast hump of camel."

"Ooh, yes," said Ivy. "I've never had the hump."

"Oh, trust me, you can't beat a good hump," said Ned.

Sylvia was frantically flicking through the menu, turning it upside down, turning it round, looking for the exotic dishes she'd missed. Ned chuckled and continued.

"Or perhaps the saddle of mule. Would you like a huge ass, Ivy?"

She beamed, grateful for the set-up.

"No thanks, I've already got one."

He set down his menu and mimed squeezing her buttocks.

"Not too big for my hands."

She didn't even go red.

"I think I have the wrong menu," said Sylvia. "You must have the à la carte."

The atmosphere was set for the rest of the meal, and the wine only added to the light-hearted merriment and relaxed chit-chat. Sylvia couldn't quite figure out what was going on but was sure things were going well. She could tell by the way Ned and Ivy were laughing and bouncing jokes off one another. It didn't matter that she couldn't keep up with them.

So they were all pleasantly tipsy at half past three as they finally made their way back to the office. The brightness of the outdoors combined with the alcohol to lend the world a slight unreality; Ivy thought it dreamlike, but a dream in which she felt compelled to laugh, and she rarely had dreams like that.

"I'm not normally a fan of that sort of place," said Ned as they strolled three abreast along Colmore Row. Ivy sensed Sylvia's disappointment at this confession, but also that Ned was either unaware or didn't give a damn. "But I have to say that if you have the right company, it can make up for any amount of pretentious arse." This seemed to perk Sylvia up. She thought Ned was referring to her company.

"I don't mind them too much," said Ivy, keeping things upbeat. "As long as the food is fresh and the place is clean, I'll give anything a go."

Ned arched an eyebrow.

"What's that old Magyar blessing? May your food be fresh, your drink be strong, your cock be long, and your women open-minded."

"Ned!" Sylvia shrieked. "You can't say that in mixed company." She was trying to overreact playfully, still flattering herself that Ned was directing his sentences at her as much as at Ivy.

"Why not?" He spoke to Sylvia but looked at Ivy. "Ivy's an open-minded woman, aren't you, Ivy?"

She didn't want to nod too keenly, and she could tell from the underlying seriousness of his voice and from his steady gaze that he wasn't indifferent to her response. She fixed him unwaveringly and gave the slightest of mischievous smiles.

"Dangerously open-minded," she said.

"Well, yes," said Sylvia. "Me too, of course, but still, Ned … really . . ."

Ned lost his patience. He stopped walking and turned abruptly to face Sylvia.

"Do stop fussing, Sylvia. I wanted this to be a useful, informal, getting-to-know-each-other meal, and it doesn't help if you're hectoring and whining."

"Oh."

The intemperate character of Ned's rebuke stopped the party in its tracks. It threatened to sour the afternoon. Sylvia looked mortified, and Ned wouldn't be able to rescue the situation after such an outburst. Ivy could see they faced the prospect of walking the rest of the way back in silence if she didn't say something.

"Now, Ned. Don't be so harsh." She took his arm, daringly, she imagined. "I think Sylvia was only trying to protect me—my innocent ears—from your ribald and excessively male humour. Isn't that right, Sylvia?

Sylvia opened her mouth—like a goldfish—but Ivy wasn't finished.

"What she forgets, of course, is that the sort of work I've been doing for you, for the Foundation, has exposed me to far more horrific and blood-curdling forms of conduct than you could ever imagine or perform in my presence. She has no idea at all how much it takes to shock me."

This was a smart move, she thought. Laying her cards on the table at the same time as patching things up between them all. The white wine hadn't entirely blunted her rhetorical skills.

And it gave Ned a chance to get a grip, too. The wine had made him irritable. Ivy's words were an emollient. He resiled.

"*Tu as raison, naturellement*," he said. "I didn't mean to be rude, Sylvia. I'm sorry. It was a delightful afternoon, fruitfully and boozily spent. Thank you both."

"You're very welcome," said Ivy. "And thank you for taking care of the bill."

He smiled. That was reassuring.

"No need to thank me. The Foundation paid for it. After all, it was research, was it not? Finding out about one another."

"That's the sort of research I could do on a regular basis," Ivy said.

They resumed their progress towards the office simultaneously. It wasn't long before Ned spoke again.

"I'm glad you said that." He put a finger to his lips, pensively, before continuing. "I have an invitation to extend to you ... both of you. We're having a bit of a get-together at the old man's place, this weekend. Saturday afternoon. Nothing spectacular. Just a barbecue and some music. Mostly people from the church."

Ned hadn't struck Ivy as religious. Was that going to be an obstacle? In truth, she didn't really know how she felt about it; she thought she'd better find out more.

"The church?"

He gave her a queer look, querying her query.

"Sylvia didn't mention it? The old man's church?" He exchanged glances with Sylvia.

"I didn't think it was relevant. It didn't crop up in conversation," said Sylvia meekly.

He didn't respond straightaway, and Ivy thought for a moment that things could turn bad again. But then he shrugged.

"I suppose it isn't that relevant." He faced Ivy. "In addition to funding the Hartfield Foundation, my father is the head of a small religious community, the Transcendental Gospel Crusade. Bit of a Bible thumper of sorts, I suppose. Quite the character. Still, he's a decent enough old cove, and I suspect, Miss Feckett, you'll find him ... what? ... intriguing. Besides, it might give you a chance to network. He can be a valuable man to know if you're looking to develop a career in the world of philanthropic foundations."

It sounded harmless enough.

"You have my interest," Ivy confessed. "Can I bring Sam along?"

It was an innocent question, but it stalled their progress once more.

"Sam? Who's he?"

"My assistant. My partner."

Ned's face fell.

"Partner?"

"Research partner, research partner," she said, quickly divining the source of his concern. "Nothing else ... well, he's a friend, too, but not ..."

He nodded but said nothing. Ivy wondered whether she'd spoiled things.

"Of course you can, Ivy," he finally said. "Please. Any friend of yours must have excellent taste. I'm sure he's a lovely chap."

"He is, Ned, he is," she said, relieved. "I value him very highly ..." She broke off in mid-sentence to engage him meaningfully and to emphasize her final words.

"As a researcher, I mean."

Chapter Eight

Shops may close and businesses fold, but there will always be work for an alchemist.
St. Nidri's Phonecall to the Cherokees 5:9

The headquarters of the Transcendental Gospel Crusade, referred to as the Tabernacle despite being neither a tent nor mobile, was formerly a boys-only preparatory school close to Solihull town centre. It also functioned as the home of George and Valerie Hartfield, Ned's parents; prior to the establishment of the Crusade, that had been its only function, George and Valerie having purchased the building from the local council after the school had run into financial difficulties.

The standard version of the founding myth was that not long after moving into the building, George made the fateful discovery that was to change his life—and those of his family—forever when he whimsically investigated the contents of several cardboard boxes marked "Heinz Mulligatawny Soup," found the day he decided to shift Ned's childhood memorabilia into the attic.

There was no clue as to who had packed these boxes or stored them away; the cardboard was well worn, although of recent origin, but the contents—and George was expert enough to recognize as much—dated back to the 16th century. His familiarity with Latin and fluency in classical Greek (he had been a student at Solihull School decades before and had studied Archaeology and Business Administration at Durham in the 1950s), in concert with his native curiosity, self-discipline, and business acumen, motivated him to translate the long-lost scriptures, for that is what they were, in their entirety and to prepare a media presentation package to promote his discovery to the best advantage.

As a consequence, when the bow-tied doorman greeted them that Saturday afternoon, Sam and Ivy saw not only the inside of a private school for the first time, but also a well-oiled, media-friendly, healthily financed religious organization, a sort of Plymouth Brethren for the Birmingham Bourgeoisie.

"That eye-of-the-needle routine is evidently old hat," Sam whispered as they entered the foyer, and then, "Bloody hell, it's massive," as he took in the main auditorium directly ahead.

"There must be seating for hundreds in there."

"Five hundred and fifty, actually."

It was Ned's voice. He'd snuck up behind them, having observed their entry and weighed up the right approach.

"Ned," said Ivy.

"Good to see you, Ivy. Thank you for coming. You're bang on time, just as I expected. This gentleman must be Sam." He extended his hand.

"Pleasure to meet yow. I didn't realize this place was so big."

"My father will tell you that it's all God's doing, Sam, but the truth is that it's the result of perspiration. Lots of it. And maybe *some* inspiration."

"Divine inspiration, though, surely?" said Ivy, wanting to keep the conversation light. "That can go a long way."

"Indeed it can," Ned agreed. "Do you want to come through and meet the rest?" He winked at Ivy. "Sylvia's already here ... no surprise. You just have to sign in here, if you wouldn't mind." He indicated a guest book. "Put down your e-mail address for regular updates of our activities." Sam smirked in Ivy's direction at the very thought, but when she pursed her lips and gave her "don't embarrass me" glare, he took the pen that Ned proffered and meekly signed the book.

Formalities completed, Ned led them along a broad, light corridor running off and then parallel to the auditorium, towards the back of the building. Ivy spent the brief journey checking out Ned's thighs, his behind, his haircut, tamed into neatness for the day, and his gait, at once confident and relaxed. And his shoes. Paul Church. Flawless and appropriate, Ivy joked to herself.

Sam's attention was not so one-tracked. He was checking out the images on the corridor walls, portraits and photographs of individuals who had been influential in the church's history or who played a part in its theology. He was struck by how few he recognized, and before they reached the grounds behind the building, his curiosity got the better of him.

"Ned, I'm sorry." He had found it difficult to keep up with Ned's stride. "Can I just ask you? Who was Saint Theophobe? I don't think I've ever heard of him. Or Saint Tatrius. Who was he?"

Ned's patience was rather better that day, though he'd been trying to force the pace precisely to avoid questions like this. Ivy reflected that perhaps it had been a mistake to bring Sam. She trusted his opinions, by and large, but she could see now how he could be a liability in her pursuit of Ned.

"I'm not surprised, to be honest," said Ned, a slight tone of condescension entering his voice. "They are, however, highly revered figures within my father's house, if you'll forgive the pun. Their stories are told in the revealed scriptures: The Book of Telethon, to be precise."

"Tele—" Sam was barely half-way through expressing his scepticism before he got a hard kick on the shin from Ivy.

"They were martyred in 347 A.D. for their proselytizing of the New Covenant," Ned continued. "They were impaled on stakes outside the walls of Thermopylae." A brief nod of understanding was all that Sam allowed himself. "But listen, you'll learn more about that sort of thing from my father. He's the head honcho round here when it comes to scripture. Ask him. You're here to have a good time and meet the folks, right?"

Was that so? She was here to meet the folks? Maybe things were moving along more quickly than Ivy had anticipated. For goodness' sake, they hadn't even exchanged so much as a friendly kiss, and here she was about to be introduced to Ned's parents. She couldn't help but think it a bit old fashioned, and maybe a bit presumptuous, too, but sometimes these religious movements were wary of outsiders, so perhaps there was cause for the Head and Mrs. Honcho to take an interest in their son's extracurricular activities.

At the rear of the Tabernacle, two score or so of the Hartfields' most devoted and/or influential congregants gathered in small groups of grins and carefree conviviality. Ivy recognized, thanks to her research, two former mayors of the borough and a onetime chief of the West Midlands police force, while Sam spotted a married couple from the upper echelons of the BBC, based in Pebble Mill, and one of the country's least liked arms manufacturers, someone whom, given Ivy's recent work, she ought to have identified straightaway. In addition to these high-fliers, there was a manager of one of Birmingham's professional football clubs, a director of one of the others, two regional shopping magnates, and one Miss Walsall City Centre 1998.

"What would madam like to drink?" An amiable, bald-headed waiter of Ivy's own height was holding a notepad inches from her chest.

"Oh ... a white wine, please."

He duly noted the request and switched his attention to Sam, who, trying to be difficult, ordered a Mackeson.

"Would that be a half or a pint, sir?" came the unflustered, unimpressed reply.

"Just a half," Sam said, sheepishly. "Please."

The moment the waiter departed, Sam felt the need to avenge the petty humiliation.

"Quite a freewheeling deal they've got going here, Vee, isn't it? Just look at all that booze over there behind the counter. They don't seem to worry too much about abstinence, do they?"

"You don't know that." She was determined to stick up for Ned. "This might be a religious festival of some description for all you know. Getting drunk once a year and then abstaining from alcohol for the other 364 days. Just have the decency not to pass judgement out loud. You *are* a guest, remember."

Suitably chastened, Sam bit his lip. It was clear that the invitation carried more importance to Ivy than it did for him. Perhaps she was thinking of the job opportunities it might afford her. For her sake, he resolved to keep schtum.

The waiter returned with their drinks, and Ned approached with his mother, a tall, angular, well-dressed woman in, Ivy estimated, her mid-fifties, although the lines around her taut and pinched mouth betrayed years of tobacco addiction. Even before Ned introduced them, Ivy could sense that his mother was scrutinizing her, looking her over for chinks in her armour. And Ivy had no armour.

"It's a pleasure to meet you, Mrs. Hartfield. You have a lovely home."

"It isn't often you get an invitation to somewhere like this, I would imagine."

Her voice was like her face. Strained. Sour.

"It certainly isn't, no. Thank you very much."

She took the gratitude as read. There was no graciousness about her.

"Mom's a marvellous entertainer," Ned gushed. She shot him the briefest of smiles for the compliment.

"Really?" said Ivy. "Do you sing or tell jokes?"

She looked at Ivy with the sort of horrified sneer that Nigel Farage reserved for "abroad."

"No," said Ned, close to an outright guffaw. "I mean entertaining in the sense of being a hostess. Holding parties and suchlike."

Ivy felt her stomach plummet down a liftshaft of embarrassment. She wanted to say, "Oh fuck," and would have, had she been there on her own. Several hours later, when she lay in her bed and remembered the day's events, she would indeed say out loud, "Oh fuck," but that was mostly because she'd had too much white wine.

"How silly of me. Of course, that's what you meant," was the best she could manage, imagining quite naively that demeaning herself before such a vicious woman would earn her something other than increased contempt.

Fortunately for Ivy, she was rescued from further humiliation by a rather weird apparition. He glided through the throng as though carried aloft by angels; the crowd obscured Ivy's view so that all she could see was the upper torso and head of Ned's father. What was most astonishing was not the size of his head—like a pink basketball, Ivy thought— nor the spiral of pure white hair poised majestically atop his pate like a coiled whip of ice cream inclined precariously to the left, so that Ivy expected it to slide off at any moment. No, what startled her most of all was that George Hartfield was a good foot and a half taller than everyone else around him. All those clapping, cheering, hallelujahing fans, they *literally* looked up to him, and it wasn't until he made his way around the outside of the crowd and up onto the small platform especially erected for the day's festivities, gliding up there, smoothly, effortlessly, that Ivy understood why. He had come equipped with his very own pulpit.

During a visit to the States four years ago to attend the Southern Baptist Convention annual conference as an observer, George had, quite by chance, seen a TV advertisement for the Segway, best described as a kiddies' scooter for adults, except motorized and on sale in a country where the average exercise regimen consists of the walk from the fridge to the sofa. While the Segway didn't exactly set the world on fire (even Americans drew the line at the complete abolition of walking), George Hartfield saw in this newfangled gizmo another possibility, namely, a mobile pulpit, a way of turning any location into a venue for preaching, evangelizing, proselytizing, or otherwise presenting the message of the Transcendental Gospel Crusade to the unenlightened. What he also saw, from a psychological perspective, was a way of dominating any conversation.

The adulation had barely subsided before he began to speak and Ivy discovered whence Ned had inherited his vocal cords.

"By jingo, a man's spirit is moved by the presence of that which behooves unto him," he said.

As one, the audience gave the response.

"Kelso 3:15."

"And thus did he come amongst them to warn of the arrogance of the Beast, the confusion in the lands of Mithras, and the forging of a new covenant with Man."

Again, they replied as one, including Ned, Ivy saw. "Insults 5:26."

"And did he also go unto them and signify that that which had been promised, not least the prophecy of the false testament, had been transcended and had come to pass."

"Silloth 19:73."

At which point, the entire crowd broke into frenzied cheering and clapping and dancing and kissing and hugging. Tears of joy fell from their eyes. Breathless laughs escaped their throats like confetti. All were consumed by rapture. All, that is, except for George Hartfield, who stood above the melée and smiled benignly.

And all except for Sam and Ivy, too, neither of whom had any idea what had just happened, though it looked like fun. And until Ned, who had hugged and kissed practically everyone else, turned his attention to Ivy. He towered over her, and yet she felt no nervousness at all. If anything, it made her feel safe. And when he placed his hands around her waist and lifted her up off the ground and kissed her full on the lips, she could tell it wasn't a religious kiss. Not the way people normally kiss in church.

He drew his face away from hers and looked her in the eyes. There was a definite twinkle. And when he said, "At last, an excuse to kiss you," she nearly wet her pants.

Chapter Nine

And discovered she not the secret of the hedgehog.
                                             Plumules 3:19

Sam's emotions were all over the place the next day as he and Ivy rode out to Tudor Grange Park on another geocaching quest. On the one hand, there had been an overwhelming triumph the night before in a game of Martha Stewart Lying, the business ethics board game. In addition, he had received an invitation to join a new site for the "crème de la crème" of West Midlands geocachers, acceptance of which had resulted in the immediate notification of a previously unknown cache location. Sam was fairly confident of being on top of the caching situation in Birmingham, knowing if not the identities, at least the handles, of the vast majority of other cachers, as well as the locations of all the caches in Solihull. The chance to be the FTF was something he took very seriously, and the chance to be FTF of a cache targeted at the crème de la crème was a rare treat, one that would establish Sam as a cacher to be reckoned with. It would put him on the map, so to speak.

On the other hand, there was that kiss. Sam's senses were unnaturally heightened, not just by the excitement of the day's pursuit but also by a state of nervous energy, of an acute alertness for any sign that Ned's enthusiasm for Ivy was reciprocated. Before the party, he'd had no inkling that there could be anything between Ivy and Ned, but now ... now he was jealous. There was no other word for it.

And possessive. That too. A feeling that came as an eye-opener to Sam, who had never recognized within himself the presumption that Ivy belonged to him. Rather upsetting and guilt inducing as well, since he was such an ardent feminist. It stung him that he could have this backward-looking, Neanderthal attitude buried not so far beneath the surface, called forth by something as innocuous as a kiss on the lips.

But it didn't sting as much as the thought of Ivy belonging to somebody else.

They parked the Durköpp in the car park by the swimming baths and ambled round by the athletics track. Sam checked the GPS unit.

"I'm sure it's going to be in the Dell somewhere," he opined. "On the site, there was a coded clue I deciphered." He double-checked the co-ordinates. "Yup." He headed in the direction of the small clump of trees. "I'm surprised that this one should be so simple, to be honest."

But in truth, he was quietly pleased. They could get this thing over with and go home. He didn't feel angry with Ivy, exactly, but their conversation lacked sparkle that day. Vivacity.

"I expected this cacher to be experienced at concealment." He threw the observation her way, but Ivy wasn't paying attention. She'd been trailing behind and had barely noticed the virulence of Sam's strides across the park. She'd been oblivious to all manifestation of animus, simply because for the past twenty hours or so she'd been floating. Floating, smiling moronically, and thinking about Ned. She'd barely eaten, she was dehydrated from having taken nothing but two glasses of wine the night before, when she was so roundly thumped at the board game over at Nana's, and despite nearly weeing copiously when Ned kissed her, she hadn't even been to the loo. Nothing, in short, could distract her from the object of her affection, her new obsession.

Obsession it was, but at least for once it was a harmless one. Previous obsessions for Ivy had included turning the bathroom light on and off 116 times before climbing into the bath, filling and emptying the bath twice before getting in, blinking thirty times whenever she thought of Hitler and something her doctor had defined as triskodecafrancolinophobia: the fear of thirteen pieces of French string (it's a long story). Suffice to say that this latest obsession was sane by comparison. She used to take a lot of cold baths in the old days. When she could be bothered taking a bath at all.

It might have been nothing more than an innocent infatuation, but her fixation on Ned was nevertheless a real advance, especially if it kept her mind off Hitler.

"Well, that's a disappointment. It's not even trying."

Sam had located the cache before entering the Dell. The box was bright blue and visible from yards away. There'd been no effort to camouflage, disguise, or hide it.

"I'm amazed it's still here. Fancy leaving it out for everyone to see like that."

Ivy tried to share Sam's irritation but couldn't locate negative words in her vocabulary, so said nothing.

"Yow can expect other cachers to treat it with respect, but if yow don't hide it from the muggles they'll bugger off with it."

He lifted up the box and pulled off the lid.

"At least it hasn't been robbed. Only because it's a brand new cache, mind."

He pulled out the log book and eagerly checked for other names. He was elated to find it empty.

"FTF, Vee! First to Find! Bloody miracle if yow ask me."

With the neatest handwriting he could muster in the outdoors, Sam carefully signed his handle in the first column, first row, of the logbook before placing it back in the box and extracting the first item for Ivy's consideration. An old Action Man, in a deep sea diving suit.

"Want a new man in your life?" He couldn't resist.

The insinuation passed her by completely. She wrinkled her nose in disdain and shook her head once. Sam returned it to the box.

"Got anything needs screwing?"

He held up a six-inch screwdriver. That was no good. They'd already got a screwdriver set from the last cache. Some indication, Ivy thought, of the lack of imagination among cachers, not to mention a lack of consideration. What if a pet dog had chanced upon the box? It could have been hurt.

"How do you feel about balls?"

He extracted a packet of Panini football stickers.

"Chelsea. Not even a decent side."

He didn't need to wait for Ivy's verdict.

"That just leaves this … whatever it is."

He pulled out the final item and passed it across to Ivy.

She had to hold it up close to make it out. At first she thought it was a coin, a foreign coin like a euro or something, but it lacked the mass of a metal object, and when she scratched it with her fingertip, she felt a warmth that she associated with clay. On the first side she examined she could make out a head, as one might expect on a coin, but rather than being in profile, the head was looking out at the handler, at Ivy. Well, not looking, actually, because the eyes were hidden by a blindfold, like the eyes of Justice.

She flipped it over. It was fiddly to hold, but she managed to pinch it between forefinger and thumb. On the other side, there was a single letter. A capital M. Or a W. It wasn't clear which. Maybe it referred to the figure on the other side, Ivy conjectured. Or the year 2000.

"Looks like some sort of counter," she suggested.

"Counter or counterfeit." She refused to acknowledge such a feeble joke.

"I guess that's the keeper," she said. Let's find out what it is."

Sam nodded, and as he dug his centipede from his coat pocket, Ivy retrieved her purse from deep inside her duffle coat and secreted the counter within.

"Not much of an adventure for us this week, eh?" Sam said as he sealed the lid and placed the box into longer grass.

"Not really, Sam, no."

But Ivy had never considered these Sunday mornings out with Sam to be adventures. That was just his imagination. She knew what an adventure was. And with whom she was going to have it.

It wasn't Sam.

Chapter Ten

And the word was with man. It was a very long word.
Mollusc 5:33

"I know it's short notice, but what are you doing this evening?"

There was a hint of regret in Ned's voice, but Ivy couldn't have been happier to have been on the receiving end of this question. She'd been hoping to bump into him that Monday morning, accidentally-deliberately, simply because she needed confirmation that that kiss had meant what she thought it did, and because she hadn't seen him for … what … an entire 40 hours and 17 minutes (she worked it out afterwards).

"That's okay. Monday nights are good for me." So was every other night, except maybe Saturday. "Usually I'm recovering from the excesses of the weekend."

A wry smile.

"Getting an early night to catch up on your beauty sleep, I'll wager."

She took it as a compliment.

"Something like that."

"Well, look. I'm not sure if this is the sort of thing that would interest you, but I have two tickets here for a poetry reading at the Town Hall this evening. The old man was presented with them at the weekend, but he can't go and figured I might make some use of them. I thought of you straightaway."

"Because you thought I'd like poetry?"

He lowered his face shyly.

"No. I just thought of you straightaway."

She was used to seeing him behave more assertively and with greater self-confidence. Here he was, asking her out on a date, and for the first time she was seeing him exhibit some vulnerability. How wonderful.

"Who's giving the reading?"

"Oh." He fumbled inside his blazer for the tickets. "Here we are. Yevgeny Yevtushenko. A Russian, so my father tells me. Haven't heard of him, myself."

"Are you serious? Yevtushenko is reading this evening in Birmingham?"

He double-checked the tickets.

"Yes. Is that good?"

"Ned, that is marvellous! Yevtushenko is one of Russia's ... one of the world's greatest living poets." She wanted to do a jig of delight but contained herself. She didn't know him well enough yet to be sure how he'd respond to a sight like that.

"That's great then. Can I assume that you would accede to accompanying me to the aforementioned event?"

"I'd be thrilled to. I mean, you can, yes. You can."

———

She didn't get much work done that day, and Sam didn't get much peace. She went on and on about what a wonderful poet Yevtushenko was—she'd studied Russian at school and some of his poems had been on the curriculum, so for Ivy this was tantamount to a brush with history. To see the great Yevtushenko! Sam was happy for her, naturally, but he couldn't share her enthusiasm. He'd never studied Russian, and he'd been caught on the hop by Ned, who'd had the good fortune, if not the foresight, to obtain the tickets. It was of no comfort to Sam to reflect that, even if he *had* known in advance that Yevtushenko was reading that evening, he probably wouldn't have bothered his arse to get tickets for himself and Ivy. It would only have confirmed the unpalatable truth that his resentment of Ned stemmed mostly from the fact that his appearance on the scene meant that Sam would have to make more of an effort.

"Bugger," is what he said.

Ivy snuck out of work for an early train home so she'd have time to do herself up. Neither of the girls was back at the house when she arrived—Siobhan was in Frankfurt for the night and Maggie was 33,000 feet over the Baltic—so Ivy had to rely on her own judgement when it came to choice of clothes and acreage of makeup. What was one to wear to a poetry reading in any case? And what was the appropriate level of sluttishness for a first date with one's boss? She didn't have much time to decide nor, more to the point, much experience, so she erred on the side of caution, reasoning that rapid progress had been made thus far without her having to do too much out of the ordinary. She plumped for pale pink lipstick, skipped the eyeliner but pinched some of Maggie's mascara from the bathroom, and spritzed herself with some Fendi eau de toilette that Siobhan seemed to have forgotten was in the cabinet (Siobhan had briefly dated a vegan who'd thrown a wobbler over her choice of a scent carrying a furrier's marque). A long skirt might be a bit of cliché for a poetry reading, she thought. It conjured up images of dowdy, bun-haired librarians with flat shoes and no sense of humour. But then she also reasoned that glamour and poetry made for curious bedfellows and that Yevtushenko was likely to be pretty intense here and there, so she contemplated the trouser suit again before recalling she'd worn it the first time she met Ned, and she couldn't have him thinking she was that hard up for clothes.

What to do, what to do.

Suddenly, she hit upon the answer. Jeans. She had jeans. Remember what Ned said about women in trousers. Perfect. And jeans told Ned that she wasn't going to make too much of an effort to impress him. It was his job to do the impressing. Granted, she already *was* impressed, but not enough. Yet. Besides, jeans also said she was comfortable attending poetry readings, that she was someone more concerned with lofty, abstract, intellectual matters than ornamentation and self-adornment. And jeans also disguised, she hoped, the fact that she was deranged to the point of incontinence that this might be the most important night of her life thus far.

———

Yevtushenko was getting on a bit, she had to concede, and not having seen photographs of him before, she was surprised that he was so slight. Slight, but still a handsome man, with a warm, friendly smile and piercing, intelligent eyes, which, when he read, glowed with embers of wit that warmed you to him, carried you with him. He wasn't just a poet. He was a performer, a conjurer of never-before-imagined worlds so real that you could touch them, taste them, and see them for yourself.

It was not just Yevtushenko who exceeded Ivy's expectations; the audience did, too. The place was packed. Packed with librarians and schoolteachers. How sad for Yevtushenko, she thought, to be so famous but to have your entire fan club composed of these sexless, emotionally repressed wallflowers. How he must long for voluptuous, sumptuous, moist-lipped nymphomaniacs sitting in the front row, crossing and uncrossing legs the length of a Birmingham Sunday, blowing him kisses and writing their phone numbers on their knickers and tossing them onto the stage. She felt positively fecund by comparison. She was one of the very few women there to have male company. It was a room that made Ivy feel like a sexbomb. She wished the reading could have lasted forever.

They came out of the Town Hall into a still, warm night and stood at the top of the stone steps.

"Shall we go for a drink?" Ned suggested. "A nightcap?"

"I'd better not. I have to work tomorrow, and the last train goes at quarter past. Besides, my boss is a real martinet."

"He clearly doesn't know how to treat you. I, by contrast, am determined that you will not be going home by public transport tonight. We'll get ourselves a taxi."

Ivy pulled away.

"No, really. I can't afford it. And I have a season ticket for the train."

"It won't cost you anything. I would have taken a cab in any case. You may as well travel back with me. We don't live that far apart."

He reached for her hand.

"How unchivalrous of me would it be to let you go home unaccompanied?"

He had a point.

"And on public transport, too." He frowned theatrically. "Utterly unthinkable."

He squeezed her fingers gently, a silent encouragement. He'd been the perfect gentleman all evening, she decided. He wasn't going to try anything funny.

"If you insist, you can drop me off outside the train station in Solihull. That way, we're compromising. How about that?"

He accepted with a small, angled nod, and she squeezed his hand in return.

She didn't let go until Solihull.

Chapter Eleven

Ask not of him with no eardrum whether the falling tree makes noise. It disturbs the airwaves around him, but with no eardrum, there is no noise. Besides, he can't hear you ask the question.

Dilemmas 7:8

It was on the day after Ivy's date with Ned that the first of a number of peculiar occurrences took place in her life. Or, I should say, not so much *in* her life but in the world around her, in her immediate vicinity. Taken in isolation, each of these occurrences might have struck anyone witnessing it as an unfortunate calamity or a freak accident, worth recounting to friends and family once they got home but having no ramifications beyond that. For someone seeing all of them, however, an omniscient narrator, say, the possibility that their connection to our newly enamoured spinster might be no more than coincidental could not be countenanced for more than a moment, unless one was attempting a trip to the farther shores of the surrealist imaginary.

The journey from her front door to the bottom of Broad Oaks Road that next morning was taken up by her preoccupation with Ned's tongue and the sound of Ludovico Einaudi. She'd let Ned continue on his trip home to Rectory Road the night before (his place was only round the corner from the Tabernacle) without inviting him in for coffee.

That he'd paid for the ride home didn't in Ivy's eyes entail any obligation on her part, and she was sure he wouldn't have been indiscreet enough to try to finagle his way in; she'd merely wanted to maintain some decorum, and, if she was honest, the decision had more to do with not being able to trust herself with him than the other way round.

Hence, they had separated outside Solihull train station, as agreed, but before being separated, they had been conjoined.

"Thank you for accompanying me this evening, Ivy. I wouldn't have enjoyed it half as much had I gone on my own or ..." he feigned a shudder, "if I'd invited Sylvia."

Ivy snickered.

"I'd like to express my gratitude, if I may, by extending a further invitation. My place, Saturday night, dinner? I'm having a few friends over, just a handful, and I think you will get on with them famously. My culinary skills leave something to be desired, I confess; it'll be spag bol and Viennetta. But the company will compensate. Especially if you come."

She was yet to release his hand at that point. Now she found herself examining it, then stroking it.

"I'd be delighted, Ned. The pleasure will be all mine."

He grinned.

"I assure you it won't, but I'll do everything in my power to ensure you have all the pleasure you want."

She took this to be the thoroughly ham-fisted attempt at insinuation that it was and raised her face to his.

"Have you got what it takes, do you think?"

Their mouths were inches apart. She felt herself exhale into his mouth as she completed the question. His response was swift but tender.

"I can only try my best."

It was an awkward kiss, not least because of the significant difference in their heights. Ned was bending from the waist as far as he could, while Ivy craned her neck up and back so that her open mouth was nearly horizontal, her tongue reaching for the stars. It might have been easier for Ned to bend his legs and crouch, but it would have looked even more comical, and no man stoops like that to kiss someone unless he's giving his little niece a peck on the cheek. Crouching and French kissing at the same time is just weird.

So Ivy faced the sky and kissed him, let her mouth be filled, happily, gratefully, with a lump of alien flesh; like a tumour, she thought, like raw liver, but moving, searching, living and powerful. She accepted it despite its strange texture and she licked it, sucked it, caressed it with her own tongue, curled her own tongue around it, welcomed it, drew it in. She had never kissed like this before, nor been kissed like this. And she realized for the first time what it meant to be in love. It meant to no longer be oneself. It meant, in her best postmodern academic jargon, to accommodate the alien, the foreign, the Other. That to love is to reach out beyond yourself, beyond the familiar. It meant to taste the world, to join the world, and at the same time let the world taste you.

At least, that was the conclusion she was coming to as she reached the far side of the pedestrian crossing at Streetsbrook Road the next morning, a conclusion that filled her with glee, made her feel ethereal, joyous, a part of the world, a feeling quite distinct from the usual anxiety that skewered her like an ice-cold lemon-juice enema any time she thought of the scarcity of human intimacy in her life. She was ecstatic to the point of distraction.

To the point that she failed to notice the pager clipped onto her belt going off, emitting its ear-piercing wail over a 20-yard radius, drowning out the moan of the Tuesday morning stream of traffic heading into Brum.

We can make the further excuse on Ivy's behalf that her iPod was cranked up and its battery working properly, so that if she hadn't been otherwise entertained by reminiscences of Ned's firm organ between her lips, the sound of Einaudi would still have sufficed to mask the insistent beeping of the pager.

Fifty-eight-year-old Reg Carter of Sharman's Cross Road was far too gauche to have encountered Einaudi's MOR genius and was possessed of opinions regarding the use of personal audio equipment that had rendered his knowledge of their evolution as outdated as the transistor radio. As a consequence, when he heard Ivy Feckett's pager go off, being blind, he mistook its sound for that of the pelican crossing another ten yards up the road from where he decided to step into fast-moving traffic.

He wouldn't have known that it was the Number 17 bus from Solihull town centre to Acocks Green that hit him, nor that it was a double decker being driven by Stuart Palmer, who'd been in the job three and a half years and had successfully shucked off the nickname "Smeggy" after improving his personal hygiene. Nor was there time to relay this information to Reg. He lapsed into unconsciousness as a result of the impact and massive internal haemorrhaging not 5/6ths of a second after being hit.

The squeal of the bus's brakes and the tremendous THUD! as Reg's body bounced off the grille turned the heads of everyone in the immediate vicinity, bar Ivy. Sue Bateley of Prospect Lane screamed hysterically just once before fainting dead away, and several concerned citizens, all men, ran over to Reg's body, determined that they be seen to be capable of assuming responsibility and acting decisively at times of crisis, but on reaching him they had no idea what to do.

Ivy did not turn. The pager cut out only seconds after the accident, and then the next Einaudi track kicked in. In addition, she'd been trying to find her season ticket in her pocket, and she was still recalling the previous night; a vague, mischievous smile had begun to play over her lips as she remembered the look of delighted surprise on Ned's face as she had withdrawn her mouth from his to plant a last kiss on his cheek.

Interestingly, this wasn't the first time Reg Carter had died. Only ten months previously, he'd suffered a major cardiac episode that required immediate emergency treatment. Luckily for him, an ambulance arrived on the scene within minutes and the defibrillator was applied, reviving

Reg, who'd been lying dead on Danford Lane for two minutes. A fortunate reprieve. But there was no coming back this time. Lazarus was well and truly gone.

This account of events is inaccurate. In fact, there were two other heads that were not turned by Reg Carter's resounding thump. One was that of a frail, grey-haired, gnarled, bandy-legged, rheumy geriatric, a man regarded as irrevocably senile by some, daft as a brush by many others. The other was that of his shiny-coated, devastatingly handsome, unaccountably good-looking companion. Their heads were not turned because they'd been watching Ivy Feckett throughout. They'd been waiting for something like this to happen all along.

Chapter Twelve

Shouldst thou want thy beloved committed, drive him to madness with thy tongue.
Lucille's Ambiguous Message to the Arabs 2:19

"I shan't be able to come round on Saturday night."

She knew the news would come as something of a surprise.

"What's the matter? Are yow getting tired of being thrashed at Swizzo!?"

"'Course not. How could one tire of that?"

By keeping the tone of the conversation jokey, she hoped to avoid any expression of disappointment.

"Nana will be very disappointed, yow know."

She'd failed. And she felt guilty, too. And annoyed at Sam for playing the 'Nana' card, reminding her of what she already knew: that she was letting down an old lady.

"Are yow going off to another poetry reading?"

He was being sarcastic.

"No, I'm not. For your information, I'm going out to dinner."

He tried to look unfazed.

"Very nice. Going out with yowr boss to some posh French gaffe, no doubt."

Clever. He was casting aspersions upon Ned's taste and at the same time fishing for information. Ivy took the bait.

"Not that it's any of your beeswax, but I'm going round to his place for a dinner party ... to meet some of his friends."

One of the junior librarians, weighed down by a pile of late-19th-century anthropological classics, struggled past but managed to cast them a disapproving glare. Ivy caught it. Sam was unswayed.

"Friends, eh? Are yow sure they're not going to be disciples? Yow might find yourself chained to the wall in his dungeon while they drip candlewax on one another, sacrifice the nephew's kittens, and dress up like goats."

He mimed goat's horns on the top of his head with his forefingers.

"It's not that sort of cult."

Ivy raised her voice despite the librarian and despite the fact that she had no idea whether it was that sort of cult or not.

"And anyway, even if it is, it'll be a change."

Sam looked offended at that insinuation, though Ivy hadn't meant anything by it—it had been said for effect rather than out of any genuine boredom at their usual Saturday night ritual. She skated over the insult by ignoring it and redoubling her own attack.

"And for your information, *that*," she mimicked Sam's goat's horns, "is the sign to indicate that someone is being cuckolded, *not* that they're dressed up like a goat."

"Is it really?" Sam said, knowing full well she was right. "So tell me then, oh wise one, what's the sign to indicate that someone is dressed up like a goat?"

She had no idea.

"Cloven hooves."

She parted her fingers like Mr. Spock from Star Trek, inverted her hand and made a vague clawing movement.

"Yow're making that up."

"Am not. That's the symbol deaf people use," she lied.

"For dressing up as a goat?"

He didn't believe a word of it.

"Yeah. With the left hand."

She made a more vigorous, downward stabbing movement for emphasis.

"And deaf people do that a lot, do they? Dress up as goats, I mean."

Ivy shrugged.

"Not all of them, obviously. That would be stupid. Just the ones in cults."

"Of course."

———

When Ivy arrived at Ned's that Saturday night, she discovered there had been a calamity. Ned, debonair to a fault, scarlet cravat neatly tied and draped with élan down his shirt, couldn't have been more apologetic.

"Roberta and John called not half an hour ago to say that their babysitter had had a row with her parents and been grounded, leaving them shorthanded and unable to find a replacement. And I've just got off the phone with Philip and Judy, who, it turns out, thought it was next

Saturday they were due to come round, and they already have Judy's parents over and her sister and her boyfriend on the way. It looks like it's just going to be the two of us, Ivy. I hope you don't mind."

"Not at all. That is so disappointing for you, though. After all the work you must have put in."

He opened the front door wider to allow her access and reached to divest her of her coat.

"I hope you like spag bol. I've plenty of it."

They ate and ate until they were stuffed; Ivy lent him a hand in the kitchen, since it was just themselves, and which made it more fun, and the bottles of Zinfandel that had originally been apportioned on the basis that the fellas would drink at least three glasses and the women maybe two, now became their exclusive property and helped them down much more of the spag bol than Ivy thought possible. And after they'd washed up, Ivy washing and Ned drying, since he knew where everything went, all the time chatting, discussing Sartre, astronomy, 14th-century troubadours, Van Morrison, Galway, Galway Keller, Helen Keller, goats, and cuckolding, they were fit only to fall down on the sofa with a brandy and then fall comfortably asleep in the warm glow of a coal fire and satisfied appetites.

And they would have done just that, had Ned not picked Ivy up off the sofa after she finished her first brandy and carried her into his bedroom.

She did not remark upon the oddity of a single man owning such a large bed: king-size. Ned was a big guy, after all, and she was woozy after all the alcohol.

Ned hadn't plied her with drink in order to get her into bed. He'd drunk as much as her, if not more, and if he had seduced her, he had done so fairly, by virtue of his conversation, his jokes, and his solicitousness, by listening to what she had to say and taking her seriously. And if Ivy had allowed herself to be seduced, she had done so freely. She would have walked into his bedroom of her own volition, and indeed could have done so, albeit wearily, had not Ned decided it would be more romantic and apt for him to convey her there himself.

While inexperienced in the techniques of the boudoir, Ivy knew enough to know that she would never be made love to again the way she was made love to that night. Perhaps the term "made love" did the scenario an injustice, however, since Ivy was not worldly enough to distinguish between the spontaneous eruption of passion that can compel a man to engage in acts of eroticism conceivably illegal, immoral, and certainly unnatural, and the pre-planned, formulaic manoeuvres of a sexual roué intent on deriving from the night a specific set of tableaux or experiences for present delectation and future recollection. All Ivy really knew was that she was thrown around the bed that night like she was some kind of rag doll. Ned's masterful hands, his muscular arms, gave him the leverage and strength to raise her from whatever position she found herself in and to rearrange her—her limbs, the orientation of her body, her attitude, and presentation— to suit whatever whim or urge took him or whatever hypothesis he wished to test.

She allowed herself to be placed, thrown, and turned over and around, and she participated, to the best of her understanding, in each project as they suggested themselves to him, because she discovered that this was not necessarily a one-sided arrangement. By allowing herself to be explored by his tongue and his fingers and his toes and his penis, she found herself delivered of sensations previously unimaginable to her. And not just sensations but also ideas. Such ideas. So vulgar and crude, in any other circumstance, yet here she found herself acting upon them instantaneously, eagerly, happily, without any reservation. She relearned what she had found out only days earlier about love: that being penetrated from the outside means also that you enclose, engulf, surround, taste, discover. That active and passive are not two opposing and contradictory sides of the same coin but that that which seems passive is simultaneously active. As Ned knelt between her legs and offered her his mouth, so she kissed him and knew the geography of his lips.

When they finally got to sleep, when they were drained, exhausted, spent, it was with Ivy's head resting on his massive, hairless chest, his arms wrapped round her shoulders, and their respective genital areas raw and dry. The erection that Ned awoke with the next morning was nothing but an inconvenience, but one that made them both laugh. There was no way either of them was going to respond to its suggestion.

Chapter Thirteen

Cast not thy spit upon the waves; the oceans know how to spit back.

Holograms 8:10

Having laughed about Ned's erection, Ivy's next action was to panic at having slept in and missed her appointment with Sam. She leapt from the bed and into her underwear in one move, scaring the wits out of Ned, who wondered what he'd done to cause such a hasty departure.

"Was it that bad?" he asked, pulling the sheet back across his torso to keep warm.

"What?"

She heard the question but didn't get the reference, occupied as she was by the search for her bra.

"Did I do something to offend you?"

They'd managed a few novel manoeuvres the previous night, but Ned hadn't been so attentive as to wonder whether Ivy was enjoying herself.

"No, not at all."

She spun around, looking around herself at the floor, for her shoes.

"I was meant to meet Sam at half-ten. We'd arranged to go out this morning."

With the benefit of hindsight, Ivy was free to wonder how mad she really was. Sitting on the bus on the way to Sam's, she reminded herself that she had just left the cozy bed and warm embrace of a sexual athlete on a wet Sunday morning in order to sit on the back of a fifty-year-old scooter with her arms wrapped round a skinny, adenoidal, post-adolescent Marvel Comics collector while they rode around Birmingham in the search for camouflaged Tupperware boxes containing three quid's worth of trinkets. Why couldn't she, just for once, have said, "Fuck Sam, I'm staying here"? Where was the incentive to leave Ned's bed? Other than the slight discomfort that all couples feel after their first night together, not to mention the physical discomfort, the aches, and the soreness, the only possible explanation had to be some form of ineluctable, inherited mental illness. She had to be genetically predisposed to insanity.

Possibly insane and yet, surprisingly, disappointed when she arrived at Sam's. Having jumped on the bus and built up a sweat running down the street in the rain, knowing she was already an hour late, she reached the driveway just as the front door opened, only to see the firm, toned figure of Caroline emerge.

"Hi Vee. What happened to you?"

"I ... I slept in ... came as fast as I could ... Is Sam in?"

"'fraid not. Gone fishing ... Slept in?"

"Yeah." Ivy was still trying to get her breath back. "Gone fishing?"

Caroline shifted her sports bag from one shoulder to the other.

"Earlswood Lakes. The Reservoir. Once he concluded you weren't coming. And you weren't answering the phone. He must have called five or six times, Vee."

Ah.

"I … er … I stayed with a friend. I was out last night … for a meal."

Ivy felt the gaze that fell on her turn from the curious to the suspicious.

"With a friend, eh?" But Caroline was polite enough not to pry further. "Sam was a bit peeved, I reckon … Because he couldn't reach you. You might want to pop up to the Reservoir and find him."

Caroline was thinking more of her own brother's feelings than the health of his relationship with Ivy, but she still managed to affect an air of universal concern.

"My bike's round the side of the house here. You can take that. I'm off to Tae kwon do. I've an exam coming up for my black belt. Putting in extra hours."

She descended the front steps and patted Ivy on the shoulder.

"Be nice to him."

"Sure, Caroline," she said, defensively. "Why wouldn't I be?"

———

Ivy wasn't at all comfortable sitting on Caroline's cycle, and she hadn't washed before leaving Ned's. What was more disconcerting, she could still smell Ned on her: his sweat, his saliva, other stuff. After leaving Ned's, she'd ran down Sam's street and now she was biking out to Earlswood in a hard summer shower. All in all, she felt rotten. Grubby.

Even though the previous night had seen the most spectacular shagging in her entire life, she hadn't had a chance to bask in the glory of it. There hadn't been time. Only when she made it off the Stratford Road and onto the Tamworth-in-Arden cycle path was she able to let her mind wander a bit.

At least then she felt warm inside as well as out. Maybe it was just her lungs burning. But she smiled anyway, vacantly, through the pain, through the rain, through muddy puddles that stained the hem of her jeans a dark-chocolate brown, as beads of water exploded on the top of her head and danced in rivulets around her brow and down her cheeks, mingling with her sweat. Her sweat and Ned's.

The warmth wasn't from her lungs, she finally decided, nor from the satisfaction of being loved, but from a sense of accomplishment. Ivy felt like she'd actually achieved something that night. She'd let herself go. She'd lost control. She'd surrendered to lust. She'd *felt* lust; how about that? That was what it was. The joy of knowing that she was capable of lust. That was what made her feel warm.

Cool.

But the sight that greeted her upon arrival at the Lakes caused her to brake sharply. Around the shoreline, as far as she could see, were umbrellas. Hundreds of them. Grey, green, black, driven into the soil. And beneath them, or behind them, or beside them, hid the middle-aged men of Birmingham.

Adjacent to each umbrella was a fishing rod, resting on a fold-out chair or some other fulcrum, and extended optimistically into the water. On the other side of each rod was a wicker basket, containing, Ivy assumed, tackle, maggots, sandwiches, flasks, the various accoutrements she imagined anglers used, though in what order or according to what routine or in what manner she had no idea.

A pair of galoshes projected beyond each umbrella, some of them crossed, others side by side, according to the wearer's mood, and here and there a cloud of pipe smoke fought to climb through the rain. Finding Sam among this lot wasn't going to be easy.

But Ivy knew Sam didn't smoke, so that eliminated at least 10 percent of the umbrellas, and she was confident she could identify him by a cough or sniff. These guys were uncannily silent, though, practically monastic in their concentration. The only sound other than the rain hitting the surface of the lake and the foliage of the trees skirting the shore was the infrequent whirr of a car passing along the causeway or the trill of a line being wound in. The atmosphere was meditative; Ivy realized, as she parked her bike and descended to the shoreline, that it reminded her of a library. She would have to approach each angler cautiously, respectfully, lest she interrupt some epoch-breaking chain of thought or, worse, scare away the fish.

She made her way along, ten, fifteen, twenty men, each of whom did no more than raise his head slowly to contemplate the intruder, offering her nothing but a stern, reproachful stare. It soon became apparent to her that she could not afford, for her own psychic comfort, to offend all those present and that she would have to find some other means of locating her quarry. If only she'd paid more attention to Sam's appearance when they went caching.

"Vee?"

His voice was at once surprised and peremptory. At first, she couldn't make out where it had come from, but when he said her name again, she spun round to see him another three umbrellas down the line.

"Sam—"

She was so pleased to find him that she'd said his name without thinking, forgetting where she was. He raised his hand in a 'halt' gesture and cut her dead. The sound of several bodies shifting in simultaneous horror at being disturbed reinforced his admonition.

"Sorry," she mouthed, and he motioned for her to come join him under his brolly.

She sat down on the other side of the handle, and he reached inside his wicker basket to find a tissue she could use to wipe her face dry. As she scraped her face with it, she asked, "Any luck?" and nodded in the direction of the lake. He shook his head.

"You?"

It was such a simple, one-word question, yet it was one she had neither anticipated nor knew how to answer. She could only offer him a feeble smile.

Sam hadn't expected an answer in any case. He was just being facetious. It hurt him that he was losing her, so he was determined to hurt her back.

He looked back out at the lake, and they sat there together, shivering, in silence.

Chapter Fourteen

If thine eye offends thee, don't look at it.
                                            Paradoxes 2:17

The next day, it was Sam's turn to miss an appointment. Unbeknownst to him, Sylvia had phoned Ivy first thing and told her she could take the day off; orders from the boss. Ivy had protested at first, unsure of her financial situation under such circumstances, but Sylvia had assured her that she'd still get paid, as per her contract, and after getting home drenched from Earlswood Lakes the previous night, Ivy wasn't going to put up much of a fight or take much persuading. It was an unprecedented decision, but she wasn't going to argue.

She phoned Nana, who told her Sam had already left for the library, and it wasn't until he got there and had logged on to one of the terminals that he gave any thought to Ivy's absence. It *did* cross his mind after half an hour of checking through the Wilson Social Sciences database that she might have caught a chill and could be stuck in bed, but he didn't try to call her before eleven, when he went out for a cappuccino and glazed doughnut. Sadly, that was ten minutes after Ivy had shut her front door and broke into a power walk in the direction of town. She was going to check out the new bookshop in the Touchwood Centre.

Fortunately for Sam, the Hartfield offices were only a quarter of an hour's walk away, so, doughnut and cappuccino in hand, he decided to pop over to see if Ivy had been delayed, had called in, or had left any messages for him as to her whereabouts. It wasn't like her not to have bothered, he thought to himself as he munched away, but then she wasn't exactly herself at the moment. She was preoccupied. Elsewhere directed. She could easily have neglected to mention that she had other plans.

The elevator doors opened onto an empty reception area. Jake was in the storeroom making photocopies of research into the syntax of the Nag Hammadi library, and because of the growling of the fan—the machine was nine years old and on its last legs—he hadn't heard the lift doors opening or Sam's hopeful hello along the corridor.

So it was Ned who was the first to respond, having heard the lift doors open from inside his office—he rarely shut the door because he had never been particularly fond of his own company and enjoyed the attention of others who might be more easily pleased.

"Ah, Sam. Good lad." Sam had forgotten how loud Ned's voice was and unconsciously took a step back. It was like the honking of a bull walrus. "What can we do for you?"

Sam pulled himself up to his full height, stiffening his back surreptitiously.

"I'm looking for Ivy. Do you know where she is?"

"Yes, of course. Which is to say, no, not exactly, but I know that Sylvia gave her the day off. Day's holiday for good behaviour."

He winked and gave a conspiratorial smile.

"I see. She didn't call to tell me."

Ned was stubbornly upbeat.

"Never mind. I'm sure she meant to. Sylvia only called her this morning, so I imagine there wasn't much opportunity. Besides, you know what women are like, eh?"

Sam acknowledged this attempt at camaraderie with the merest nod. It was enough to give Ned an entrée.

"Listen, Sam. Do you have a minute? There are a couple of things I wanted to ask you about. Would you mind?"

He stepped from behind the door to open it fully and extended an invitation for Sam to enter.

"When I say 'you know what women are like,' obviously, I'm generalizing." He shut the door behind him and cleared his throat. "What I mean to say is, you know what *Ivy* is like. That's the heart of the issue."

Sam watched him circle round to the other side of the desk, putting it between them, distancing himself at the same time as soliciting sympathy.

"I know Ivy, ahr. We went to school together."

Ned motioned for him to sit, making sure they sat simultaneously.

"Yes, I was aware of that. What I was curious about was ... how well do you know her? You're probably not aware, but she stayed over at my place the other night."

"Really?" Sam made no effort to indicate *what* he knew.

"Yes. We had a most enjoyable night."

Ned's confidence picked up as he sensed indifference on Sam's part. He took it to mean he was in no danger of assault. He pressed again to establish some masculine solidarity.

"Did you ever …?"

He left question open, but his raised eyebrows made his meaning clear.

"What?" Sam said. "With Ivy? No. Never."

Sam appeared shocked, although Ned couldn't say whether this was by the suggestion that he might have, by the thought of actually doing it, or by the frankness of the question.

"No. I thought not. Ivy said the same, but I had to check because you can't always trust them, can you? Women, I mean."

He leaned forward, across the desk, and lowered his voice as best he could.

"To be honest, I was fairly sure, just from the performance she put up. Very game, you know, but it was clear she didn't really have much idea what she was doing. I knew she wasn't a virgin fairly quickly, of course. I scored at both ends, if you get my drift. I just thought you might have been there first."

"Er. No." Sam shifted uncomfortably in his seat.

"Fair enough. I can understand that. She's not that much to look at anyway, is she, with that overbite and those little sticky-out ears? Whoever it was probably did her from behind."

Was that meant to be a joke? He had to say something.

"I'm not sure this is an appropriate subject for conversation, Ned."

Ned narrowed his eyes and sent Sam a friendly shot across the bows.

"That wouldn't be censorship you're proposing, would it, Sam?"

Right to the core of Sam's value system.

"No, no, not at all."

"And we're both men of the world, aren't we? I realize you haven't had the opportunity to sample Ivy's wares, as it were, so I'm just sharing with you ..." His voice dropped further still, to what he thought was a whisper but which for anyone else would have been a normal volume. "You're not missing out on much."

Sam's heart sank. He felt that he was now complicit in this betrayal of Ivy, this intimate exposure.

"Thank you, Ned. Thank you very much. I appreciate your telling me."

"No problem, Sam. I know you're close to her. I didn't want to tread on any toes, you understand. It makes me feel much better. Thank you for coming in."

Sam rose, backed away towards the door, and turned the handle dejectedly.

"Glad to have cleared things up," he said as he departed.

Chapter Fifteen

Isaac or Isaac substitute. Which is it to be?
Contestants 9:1

"Sam tells me you were treated to a night out last week, Ivy."

Ivy knew that Sam and Caroline had a close and trusting relationship with their Nana, but she'd never imagined it might extend to candid discussions of Ivy's personal life.

"Well ... I ... er ... yes. I was out with a gentleman friend."

"Your boss, wasn't it?"

Jesus. How much detail had they gone into?

Nana had taken the opportunity of Caroline's departure into the kitchen to make tea to get up to speed on events in Ivy's life. It was two weeks since she'd last seen Ivy, and while she was old enough to realize that people cannot be expected to exhibit consistency and reliability to the point of perfection, she'd been surprised at Ivy's absence precisely because Ivy had always struck her as someone who strove for perfection. Obsessive-compulsive, in fact. Prone to extraordinary attachments to formulae, patterns of activity, predictability, and repetition. And she had missed Ivy. Caroline and Sam afforded her great joy and entertainment, but they didn't amuse her in the way Ivy did. She felt a greater concern for Ivy, stronger maternal urges. Sam and Caroline were mentally capable, and Caroline physically, too. Nana had no qualms about letting them loose in the world. *On* the world. They were capable of looking after themselves. But Ivy, she wasn't so sure about. She still needed some supervision, some advice.

Sam had been out all afternoon at a comics convention at the NEC. He'd promised to be back before five-thirty, but it was seven now and Ivy had arrived early for their Saturday night get-together. She'd been fidgeting at home, knowing that Ned was with his folks attending to some menial church tasks—his parents were entertaining a number of Anglican clergy in order to foster ecumenical understanding, he'd told her.

The comics convention had finished at six, but Sam had fallen into conversation with two like-minded collectors, one of whom had two copies of *Howard the Duck* No. 1 in mint condition. They had repaired to a pub in Elmdon to compare notes and scoff at the ineptitude and ignorance of other conventioneers, but Sam's principal reason for delaying his return was to demonstrate to Ivy that he was no more dependent on her than she was on him, and that should she happen to forget to phone him, he'd always be able to find something to do. She needn't think he didn't have a life of his own. If he invited her to come geocaching with him, it wasn't out of desperation for company. He could find that anywhere. He invited her only because he thought she might enjoy it.

So there was Nana, sitting in her wicker chair, in her turquoise salwar kameez, shoes kicked off and a large goblet of dandelion wine immediately to hand, interrogating Ivy about the night she'd spent with Ned.

"Yes. My boss. He's very nice. Sam knows him."

"Oh yes, my dear. I know he does. He sounds like a remarkable young man. So, tell me ..."

She raised the goblet of wine to her lips and knocked back a healthy draught while Ivy dreaded the next question. How nosy was it going to be?

"... Where was it you went? The Town Hall?"

"The what?"

"The Town Hall? Sam said it was a poetry reading or a book launch or something. I can't remember exactly."

Relief poured through Ivy's body like warm honey. Yes. The poetry reading.

"That's right, Nana. It was poetry."

Caroline returned with a mug of tea for herself and a plate of Garibaldis, which she deposited deftly on the table next to the fireplace before sitting down opposite.

"And who was it you went to hear perform?"

"A Russian poet, Nana." Ivy was regaining her composure. "Yevgeny Yevtushenko. It was wonderful."

Nana reclined luxuriantly.

"Ahhh. Yevgeny. Dear Yevgeny," she said, her gaze rising to the ceiling, her mind turning his name over and over like an expensive heirloom.

"You've heard of him, Nana? I'm very impressed."

Her gaze lowered to settle on Ivy, but otherwise she remained still.

"Heard of him, child? I know Yevgeny well. Why, back in the 1960s, he used to call me his Birmingham Beatnik. 'Brumskaya Beatneetsa.' It was our little joke ... Brumskaya."

Ivy's eyes boggled.

"You *know* Yevgeny Yevtushenko?! Why didn't you go to the reading? You should have been there instead of me, Nana ... well, no, instead of Ned. He didn't have a clue who Yevtushenko was."

"Ah, Sweetness. It was all a long time ago. Before I met Sam and Caroline's grandfather. We were all very young. Very foolish." She patted down her kameez. "Pass me one of those biscuits ... thank you, dear ... Yes, Yevgeny was just becoming famous. He'd written 'Zima Railway Station' a few years before—it was the height of the cold war but people like him, like us, we were trying to generate some understanding between the two sides, build some bridges." She giggled, much to Ivy's surprise, spitting out grains of biscuit and pieces of raisin. "We did build a few bridges, all right ... between us."

"That's amazing. I'd never have thought—" Ivy had started and immediately wished she hadn't. Before she could apologize, even with a gesture, Nana had understood.

"Have thought that Nana could possibly have a life of excitement and adventure, Ivy? No, don't be embarrassed. There's no need to explain. I must seem very old, ancient, to you young ones. I'm sure the thought of me swooning over some exotic, foreign poet fills you with mirth and merriment. You find it hard to imagine that I was once a dreamy-eyed optimist who thought the world was hers to play with. But it's true. I was just like you. And you will be like me."

There was silence for a moment. Ivy didn't know what to say.

"I can think of no one I'd rather be like, Nana." Caroline found the right response. She always did. Nana blew her a kiss.

"So, Nana," said Ivy, let off the hook. "Tell us what happened?"

Nana swallowed another mouthful of wine, emptying her glass, which she held out to Caroline for refilling.

"Confidentially, dear, it just wasn't going to work out. We lived in different countries, not only far apart but separated by the Iron Curtain, too. We communicated, of course. Met up in Paris, in New York, but we both knew ..."

She looked into the middle distance, as though that was where the past was kept.

"And then, of course, I met your grandfather, and that was that."

Caroline returned a full glass to her.

"Granddad must have been very special then, to tear you away from your poet."

Nana already had another mouthful of wine. She waved her glass around in the air emphatically, whether in protest or agreement wasn't clear. Finally, she managed to swallow.

"Of course, darling, of course he was. In some ways, they were very similar. Intense. Passionate. But also, your grandfather was very correct, very disciplined. Not like me at all. You know, dear, he was so polite he'd clean his teeth before making a phone call. He was this immensely serious trade-union organizer from Glasgow. Incredibly dour. But he knew what he wanted ... and he absolutely worshipped me."

"Why wouldn't he?"

"Quite, dear." She smiled at Ivy. "In those days, I was rather exotic myself, you see. Stood out a mile. I was the only Punjabi pacifist in the Committee of 100. Men were drawn to me like moths to a flame."

The girls were nonplussed.

"What's the Committee of 100, Nana? Some sort of religious group?"

Nana almost dropped her glass.

"Honestly! Do you girls know nothing?" She shuffled forward. "The Committee of 100? The Aldermaston Marches? Bertrand Russell?" She scanned their faces. "CND? Ban the Bomb?"

"It was a very long time ago, Nana. There's more history for us to learn about now than there was for you when you were our age."

Nana's outrage gave way to a sympathetic smile at this disarming reply. She eased herself back into her chair.

"Very true, dear. Very true. That's the problem with the past, isn't it? There's so much of it. It's difficult to know where to begin, how to identify what matters ... and you have your own lives to live, too. I understand."

"You meeting granddad. That was the important bit to us, Nana. If you hadn't met him, we wouldn't be here. Tell us how that happened."

And so she did. For the next forty-five minutes, she told Caroline and Ivy all about her husband, about their meeting at a rally in Conway Hall in London, about getting arrested together during non-violent protests, about romantic meals of fish, chips, Park Drive, and pots and pots of tea in meeting rooms above pubs, and as Caroline learned about where she came from, she and Ivy both learned about the state of the world in the 1960s, about what humans were capable of threatening to do to each other, what they *did* do to each other, and where hope and optimism fitted into the scheme of things.

When Sam arrived home at 9.15, the girls and Nana were all too absorbed in the story to either scold him or show interest in his intentional tardiness. Instead, he found himself relegated to the status of observer, and it was only when the tale was well and truly completed, with the birth of their father, that Sam was indulged and allowed to open the Swizzo! box. That he won easily that night came as a hollow victory. None of the women were trying. They were too much lost in thought.

Chapter Sixteen

Salad, potatoes, bleach, toilet roll, half a pound of bacon, milk, feta cheese, ham, garlic, olives, grapefruit, bananas, brown loaf, shoe polish, Pampers.
Lists 4:21

There was an agreeable warmth to the next morning as Sam and Ivy made their way to Hockley Heath, Sam eventually bringing the Durköpp to a halt in the empty car park of The Wharf Tavern. It was still an hour before opening time, long enough, Sam calculated, for them to find the second cache to have appeared on the website, only that morning. Geocaching increased in its attractions as the summer heightened, and when someone was decent enough not only to supply new caches on a weekly basis but also to site them within the vicinity of a quality drinking hole, the rewards were compounded manifold, albeit nonintellectually.

"Down under the bridge, I reckon," said Sam, as they removed their helmets.

The pub overlooked the Stratford Canal, a lively enough route at this time of year, thanks to the tourist barges. A handful of them were moored along the wharf itself, Ivy could see; they had probably arrived the night before, their occupants envisioning a late night in the pub and a short walk home. Probably still in bed. For once, listening to the birds in the trees on the opposite side of the canal and enjoying the touch of the sun's rays on her cheeks, she did not envy them their Sunday-morning lie-in.

They walked through the car park and followed the pub terrace to the small arched bridge separating the moorings from the canal proper, where, Sam suspected, the cache was hidden. He double-checked his GPS unit and turned the map around in his hand. He'd been smart enough to print off the cache's details from the website—he'd given the pages to Ivy in order to involve her in the search. Standing on the bridge and looking up the canal, there were no obvious signs of disturbed vegetation. Rings of water erupted here and there occasionally as bream surfaced for flies, for breakfast, and when Sam and Ivy turned to look over the other side of the bridge, they disturbed an otter that disappeared under the reeds.

"Shall we go down?" Sam indicated with one finger that he meant to the water's edge.

"Why not?" she said.

Warily, they encroached onto the grass embankment, Sam first, his right hand pressing against the crumbling brick of the old bridge as he advanced, crab like, to the water.

"There's no pathway under the bridge," he called back to Ivy, who was following right behind him and thought it was stating the obvious.

He stepped down to the verge.

"Careful," Ivy advised; now she was being the obvious one. Sam peered into the shade. It was a narrow bridge, but the contrast generated by the brilliant light shining through it meant Sam couldn't see the underside.

"Any luck?"

"None at all."

"Can I have a look?"

"Go round the other side, Vee. See if yow can spot it from there."

Ivy clambered back up the embankment and jogged over the bridge to the opposite verge. She didn't have to struggle down the other embankment; she could see from where she was that there was something in the water.

"I think it's under your foot, Sam. There's a bit of twine. It goes into the canal."

"Aha!" He raised his leg and saw a cord secured between the stones by a small metal bar. Kneeling, he drew the cord up from the water with both hands, one over the other.

"Yow're right, Vee. Look what we have here."

She started back round, but Sam met her half-way, on the bridge, with what appeared to be a long, dark blue, plastic tube, one end of which had a removable lid. He shook the tube and it rattled.

"Hold out yowr hands." He pulled off the lid, and Ivy cupped her hands for him to pour out of the contents.

For the size of the tube, it was a disappointing haul. A Dinky toy—a Rolls-Royce Silver Ghost—a keyring in the shape of a human liver, a small replica pistol, and a limp, rolled-up baseball cap with the insignia of Highgate United on it.

"Christ, you can tell cachers are mostly blokes, can't you?" said Ivy.

"Not necessarily, Vee." He tried to disguise his defensiveness with an objective observation. "This is just the same cacher who hid the one in the park."

"How do you know?"

"From the website. Same handle. And ..." he had unrolled the baseball cap, "because of this." From inside the cap, he had pulled out another counter, similar to the one they'd found and kept from the previous cache.

"Is it identical?"

"No. Look." He held it out for her to examine. "It's the same on one side—it has the M or W, whichever it is—but on the other side, it's got some sort of symbol. Like one of those Hazchem symbols."

"Nuclear power, no thanks," said Ivy. "I like that." Sam handed it over.

"Yow're easy to please, Vee."

"Would you prefer the keyring in the shape of a liver?" She asked rhetorically. Then, "I wonder how many are in the set." She put the counter into her purse and Sam replaced it in the cache with his centipede. He signed the logbook—first again!—and closed the lid to return the cache to its hiding place.

At that moment, their attention was drawn to a convoy of cars pulling into the car park. It was the Hockley Harriers soccer team, third from bottom of West Warwickshire senior division 2. After every Sunday match, win or lose, usually lose, they'd reassemble at The Wharf for postmatch analysis and distribution of the blame over a pint or two of Theakstons' XB or Marstons' Pedigree, the preferred beverages for players of a certain age and the same brands imbibed the previous night in the same hostelry and therefore not only a source of consolation but also a source of the failure that necessitated consolation.

"Looks like the pub's just opening. Fancy a drink, Vee?" She pulled a face.

"Have a soft drink. Yow don't have to have alcohol. I wouldn't mind a pint."

She relented.

"Go on them. Just the one. You've got to drive home, though, remember."

The footballers were a rowdy lot. They'd managed a two-all draw, and a quick couple of phone calls had ascertained that the teams around them in the lower half of the division had fared less well, a cause for celebration. Ivy and Sam took up a position by the fireplace but soon decided it was too fine a day to stay indoors and ventured back out to the beer garden, which was still empty. The kiddies' play area was as yet unoccupied but an ever-present threat. They'd only have time for the one drink before the throngs descended.

"Can I ask you a personal question, Sam?" she said once he was half-way down his pint and loosened up.

"Three times a week," he said, trying to look blasé.

"What?"

"Whatever. Whatever the personal thing yow're going to ask me about. That's the answer I always give. Three times a week. It's never too much, never too little. Who can object to three times a week?"

"No, you daft apath. I wanted to ask you what you think about religion."

He studied her face, knowing this topic might be dangerous territory.

"Yow mean religious belief in general, or what do I think about organized religions like the Catholic Church and the Transcendental Gospel Crusade?" He said these last three words with an air of pomposity that made it quite clear what he thought.

"The first," she said, recognizing immediately the futility of asking about the second.

"Well, Vee, yow might be surprised. My attitude is one of forgiveness."

"Very funny."

"What? I know it sounds patronizing, but hear me out. All I mean is that I can understand where the religious impulse comes from." He sipped his Pedigree. "A lot of scientists, rationalists, they insist that belief in religion is irrational, that it's uncivilized, backward. But I reckon it makes perfect sense, that the source of the religious urge is rational."

"That's novel, coming from an atheist," she conceded.

"Ahr, maybe. I look at it like this: Given that this is the only universe that exists—as far as we can determine empirically, anyway—any being that attains self-consciousness will attempt to calculate the likelihood of its own existence, is going to ask itself, 'What is the likelihood of this universe, out of all those universes that could have been, that could have existed, being the one that actually exists?' And he, or she, or it, will find it impossible to calculate, because there's no answer to the question 'Why is there something rather than nothing.'"

"I see."

"Even if it's only a matter of chance, as I believe, chance is such a feeble explanation when yow think of all the things that *had* to happen for us to be here today. The zillions and zillions of events that have been necessary, that *had* to occur, in order for me to be able to sit here drinking this pint."

Ivy stroked her chin.

"In other words, Vee, *whatever* universe came into existence, if there are conscious, self-reflexive entities in it, they will be tempted to imagine that they exist for some reason, to some end. It is so totally unlikely that they would exist by chance! Which means the temptation to endow life with an objective purpose will arise wherever there are rational, self-conscious beings. It comes with the territory."

Ivy pursed her lips.

"I understand what you're saying, Sam, but that set of premises only explains why philosophy is universal, why conscious beings speculate. It doesn't explain religion. What about faith?"

"Yow're right, Vee. Yow're right. Religion arises from the tension between the belief that we must be here for a reason and the fact that bad things happen. Death, pain, torture. They all undermine our self-importance, our initial impulse to believe that our universe is special, that *we're* special. In the best of all possible worlds, bad things are happening. That's why we have religion. Faith is just the hope that there is a reason to justify the badness. Like I say, a perfectly sensible strategy, psychologically speaking."

"Hmm. Thank you, Dr. Socrates."

"My pleasure." He finished off his pint. "Now, if yow'd asked me about the Transcendental Gospel Crusade—" She cut him off.

"I didn't though, Sam, did I? I'm sure I know your views on that."

Sam felt an urgent need to repeat them, but Ivy looked like she was about to get up and walk away. He compromised.

"I was only going to say: Be careful, Vee. Don't confuse your feelings for your boyfriend, your boss, with your opinions of his church."

She sighed. "I know, I know ... Who says he's my boyfriend?"

Sam gave her a condescending smile but for all his condescension didn't know how much to tell her about his conversation with Ned. He didn't want to upset her unnecessarily but didn't want her to get hurt later either.

"You should be careful there, too, Vee. He *is* your boss as well as your boyfriend, remember. That means there's an inequality in the relationship. He exercises influence over your career prospects."

"I'm aware of that too, thank you, Sam. I'm not entirely an idiot."

She finished her pineapple juice.

"No," he said. "Not entirely." And that earned him a playful slap.

Chapter Seventeen

The angel Rafale saw Stovl and Typhoon upon the mountaintop and did blow mightily upon them. A storm shadow passed across the face of the mountain and scalped them at a distance.

Catamite & Gunsel 9:12-13

When Ivy arrived into the office the next morning, she barely recognized Sylvia. Whereas she'd previously been a riot of pink, now she was an even more major civil disturbance, only in yellow. Her hair had been dyed blonde, but a sort of artificial, lemony hue, and her matching blouse and skirt, matching each other but not her hair, had a sort of butteriness about them, except without the shine of butter, which is to say they just suggested 'fat.' All that, in addition to Sylvia's slow, deliberate movements, a consequence of the deathly hangover she was suffering, lent her an entirely new aspect: instead of the flamingo, wings flapping in a salmon sunset, she now resembled a gigantic egg yolk, rolling ponderously around the reception area.

"Ivy," she whispered. "Come in here." She pointed to her office.

"Thank you, Sylvia. Have you got your office back?" Where was Ned?

"No, no, Vee. Ned's in the conference room. He's having a meeting."

"Oh. Anything important?" She followed Sylvia into the office and shut the door.

"The vintners. And an Internet conference with a couple of the major breweries and distillers. Looks like this story will run and run."

"Do you think I should be in there?"

Sylvia wanted to show some annoyance, but it was too much effort.

"No, Vee. He didn't want you in there."

"Oh."

"It looks like we're making some progress on this issue, and your approach is too intransigent."

"Progress?"

"The breweries seem willing to consider a number of options Ned has put to them. They've been concerned for several years about declining alcohol consumption and pub use. They're looking to diversify, innovate."

"Is this all down to my letter?" Ivy felt slightly aggrieved. It sounded like the Foundation was drumming up business from her actions after dragging her over the coals for them.

"Partly, Vee. Which isn't to say you still shouldn't have sent it, but the Vintners' Association came back to the Foundation after some reflection, and Ned has been handling the matter."

"Don't I even get consulted?"

"I'm sure you will if Ned thinks it advisable. Now listen. I've set up an e-mail account for you—here is the address and the password—so you can download your assignments each week instead of having to come into the office."

"What?"

"It'll save you a journey, and you can e-mail the work back to us using the Internet facilities at the university. Savings all round."

"Will Ned ... will you want to see me from time to time to discuss how the work is going?"

Sylvia was already ushering her out of her office and in the direction of the lift.

"I'm sure we'll want to talk now and then, Ivy. That's why Ned gave you the pager, remember?"

"Well ... Can you ask Ned to call me when he's out of his meeting? There are a couple of things I wanted to ask him about."

"Of course, Ivy. I'm sure if he's not too busy, he will call. If not, you can always talk to me." She rubbed her forehead with the back of her hand and squinted. The hangover was being cruel. "I've an idea. Why don't you e-mail your questions for Ned to me, using your new e-mail account? That way, we can check whether or not it's working."

They were at the lift and Sylvia had pushed the call button. Ivy didn't get a chance to acknowledge Jake at the desk.

"I really should talk to Ned," she protested.

Sylvia didn't have time for this.

"I'll let him know you were in, Ivy. If they're matters of importance, put them in writing."

The lift arrived. It was empty. Sylvia was satisfied only when Ivy had entered and the doors had closed. But she didn't feel any better. And she certainly didn't look any better. And yellow hurt her eyes.

Chapter Eighteen

Ned didn't call.

Chapter Nineteen

And the Lord sayeth unto him: Thy destiny is written upon the water. At every moment, it changes.
Cannock 13:37

In truth, Ivy didn't have any particular topics to discuss with Ned, despite what she'd told Sylvia. She'd simply wanted to see him. But the news that the Foundation was making capital from her letter to the papers and giving her no credit for it was a good enough reason to request, no, to demand an explanation from him, she was certain, and if, at the same time, she got talk to him about, well, anything else, so much the better. She wasn't entirely sure how these things—relationships—were supposed to work, but she felt justified in the belief that a couple who had engaged in various forms of copulation might at least be expected to communicate with one another in other ways afterwards.

"There's no guarantee of that, I'm afraid, Vee." Siobhan's frank observation introduced a whole series of alternative possibilities into Ivy's frame of reference. "It depends on what the two people involved want."

They were sitting on the terrace of a small, newly opened cafe in Mell Square. Since it had been pedestrianized, the square had become Solihull's Piazza San Marco, only without canals and Doges' Palace. More 1960s than 1560s. Nevertheless, in the bright sunshine, it was a magnet for the town's beautiful people. It was the preferred pastime for

Siobhan, when she wasn't abroad, to return here and measure the fashions of the Champs-Elysées and Fifth Avenue against those of Mell Square. It made her feel like a member of the Jet Set, even if she was just one of its minions.

"You see, Vee, if you've engaged in intimate relations early on in the relationship, you're sending a pretty clear signal that you're not looking for anything long term ... unless you actually discuss it in the first few days to establish some ground rules ... where you're going. The process of getting to know someone well has more or less been bypassed under those circumstances. I'm not saying it *can't* work that way, only that you've no guarantee you're actually going to like the person, as a person, once you get to know them. At least if you're clear that it's just about sex, just a quick shag, then that's what you get, because you're both up for it, and there are no complications afterwards ... say, when you find out he supports the Albion or picks his arse. Jeez, check out those earrings."

A svelte, heavily made-up sales assistant with a Burberry scarf and gloves strolled by, the most hideous braided gold webbing swinging from her ears.

"Look like chandeliers," sighed Vee, not especially interested, focused on where she'd gone wrong with Ned.

"I'm amazed her earlobes don't reach the floor," Siobhan said. "More coffee?"

A cloud obscured the sun. Not metaphorically. Literally. But as it did, Ivy came to the realization that Ned was avoiding her.

"And what if one of the two people involved wants a relationship and the other one just wants a quick shag?"

Siobhan raised an eyebrow in surprise that Ivy couldn't work out the obvious implications of that scenario.

"Heartbreak, Vee. Chaos. Conflict. All those things that go to make up crappy romance novels."

Ivy knew once she heard it that Siobhan was right.

"But ... like ... even crappy romance novels have happy endings, don't they? I mean, I've never read one, but, everybody likes a happy ending."

"Of course they have happy endings, Vee. That's what makes them crappy. They describe a credible state of affairs and then cheat you by providing a denouement that's altogether implausible. Believe me, the chances of a happy ending other than the two protagonists finding totally new partners is very slim indeed."

Ivy nodded but wanted to cry.

"Although there is one option that might work."

"Really?"

"Two, actually. That's if one of the couple has a change of heart, decides to modify his or her intentions."

"I'm listening."

"For instance"—more coffees arrived—"Thanks. If the partner who wanted romance reconciled him or herself to the fact that it was just a quick shag, then both partners leave the relationship satisfied. End of story, of course, but happy. Alternatively, if the partner who just wanted the quick shag changed their mind and decided that the relationship was worth developing, that would give you a happy ending too."

"Okay."

"But if you ask me, that's not likely to happen unless they can be enticed into it, into seeing the relationship as something worth pursuing. The first thing that would appeal to them, that would make them return to the trough, if you'll forgive the analogy, Vee, is if the sex was really good, was *so* good that they thought it worth compromising their one-night-stand principles for."

"I see. So the first thing I would need is to be absolutely fabulous in bed."

Siobhan had known all along that they weren't talking entirely in the abstract, but Ivy's slip of the tongue still surprised her.

"You would, Vee, though I'm sure you already are."

She grinned, but Ivy didn't recognize the compliment. Siobhan realized then that their conversation was not only *not* hypothetical but also carried some urgency. She reached across the table and touched Ivy's hand.

"Vee, if you're serious about this, if you want to give this guy a chance, that's the only answer I can provide. But I can give you some pointers, too, if you like."

This was straying into territory quite foreign to Ivy. Talking sex, having sex, with men were experiences that had managed to evade her for eons, and now she was on the verge of intimate relations with a woman. She'd never had a close girlfriend, not *really* close, and now here was one ready to give her sex tips. How did one handle a situation like this? Perhaps by screwing up one's nose. She tried it.

"I don't know …"

"No, c'mon. It'll be fun. And you'll be surprised at how easy it is … how easy men are. Let's face it, they're not the most complicated of animals."

"No. That would be the Portuguese Man o' War."

"What? Yeah, right. Here, take this."

Siobhan had pulled the broad silver band off her right thumb and was holding it out to Ivy.

"Thank you. Why are you giving it to me?"

"This is what's known as a Louisiana jerk ring. I see loads of women wearing them these days, and I'm sure they're completely unaware of the origins. Try it on. They were invented by New Orleans hookers as a sex aid. When you're wanking a guy off, right, if you're doing it properly, this ring works up and down over the front ridge of his nob. They don't last more than a minute, I promise you."

"Really?"

"Yeah, so use it sparingly. The hookers use them because it increases customer turnover, if you get my meaning. More efficient."

"Thanks, Shuv."

"No problem. And here's my number one tip, Vee. Remember this, because nearly every woman gets this wrong and, let's face it, women don't read sex manuals unless they're being forced to, so pay attention. Blow jobs … it's all in the hands."

"Uh?"

"You see!? Women think you just need to know to suck rather than blow! But it isn't enough only to use your mouth. You've got to use your hand, too. You wank him with your hand and you coordinate the movement with the motions of your head."

"I see."

"You're trying to reproduce the feeling of being inside a pussy, Vee. So you have to work the full length of his cock."

Ivy started to blush at the word "cock." And then, as if things weren't graphic enough, Siobhan mimed the action with both hand and mouth, synchronized, in full view of the shoppers passing by. A spiky-haired lad in a suit caught Ivy's eye, pointed at Siobhan, and gave Ivy a thumbs-up. "Listen to her," he was saying. "She knows her stuff." Ivy was chuffed.

"Do you think we could go home and practice?" she said.

"Absolutely. We just have to stop at the greengrocer's on the way."

Chapter Twenty

*And opened he the pessary box of the Anacoluthon,
and most griev'd did it make him in the nether lands.*
Silloth 10:22

Ivy found it oddly comforting that when she turned up unannounced at the Hartfield offices that Friday afternoon, Sylvia's hair was still yellow. Never mind that her outfit was blue lamé.

"Sylvia, I have to speak to Ned. It's extremely urgent."

Ivy had prepared herself for a drawn-out campaign to get in, right down to the sombre expression on her face.

"Of course, Ivy. Just take a seat there and I'll let him know you're here. He's on the phone at the moment."

This was a turn of events she hadn't planned for. She'd pictured herself storming into Ned's office in the middle of a meeting and dictating terms, laying down the law. She'd anticipated that it would turn him on to see her so forthright, so domineering. And, of course, there was still that little matter of him stealing her glory. She hadn't to forget what she'd gone there for.

She sat there a couple of minutes, smiling politely at Jake, who gave her a wink before the phone rang and he had to answer it, and while he was chatting away Ned appeared in his doorway, looking smart in a navy blazer, white cotton Oxford shirt, and that scarlet cravat again.

He scanned the reception area until his eyes fell on Ivy. His face lit up, he opened his arms and boomed.

"I-VY! Finally! Come in! I'm so sorry we haven't got together. Please!"

She leapt from her seat with an enthusiasm she regretted. And she was disappointed in herself that she'd already forgotten how big Ned was, how much larger than life, how imposing, how loud.

"You're looking great, too," he said, as she stepped through the door he was holding. His other hand extended to shake hers, and after he shut the door, when no one could see, he leaned down, her hand still in his, and gave her a wet kiss of welcome on the cheek. Such was his tenderness and friendliness that Ivy's enmity quickly began to dissolve.

"Please, take a seat. I've been given one hell of a runaround the past week or so, let me tell you, by those buggers at the Vintners' Association. One minute they're chasing us for advice on how to implement an inclusive, non-alcohol-based integrative community atmosphere on their premises, the next they're yelling down the phone threatening to sue us for libelling the industry as racist. Honestly, Ivy, it's been a real effort to protect you, to make sure they didn't persecute one of our most trusted and valued and creative minds."

"Protect me?"

Ned held out his palms, showing her his massive, empty, clean, perfectly manicured hands.

"Of course, Ivy. What else? That had to be our priority. That's why I made sure they knew they'd have to go through me if they wanted to intimidate you. I wasn't going to tolerate that."

She'd got it all wrong. The Foundation hadn't been ripping her off. They were looking out for her.

"I thought I'd got the Foundation in trouble ... mentioning them in the letter."

He laughed.

"It wasn't the smartest thing you could have done, Ivy, but as it transpires it's allowed us to stand between you and them. I must confess, to some extent we've benefited accidentally by you mentioning us—which doesn't mean it was okay for you to do it—but in hindsight, it's worked to all our advantages."

Ivy exhaled slowly. Maybe Ned had taken some credit for her idea, but he did have a point. She wasn't entirely blameless.

"The breweries and distillers were up in arms for a while, Ivy, but I believe the Commission for Racial Equality, the Salvation Army, the British Muslim Society, and several other influential organizations saw your idea and have been ganging up on them. This is just what a think tank should be doing, Ivy: throwing out original ideas for society's benefit. It's really put the Foundation on the map."

Golly.

"And it made me realize," he said, rising from his seat, "how underappreciated you are." He came round the desk.

"I was worried you might have thought I was neglecting you, Ivy. That couldn't be further from the truth. I've been doing my best to keep you out of harm's way. I know I've been busy, inaccessible, unattainable." He squatted down beside her chair and furrowed his brow apologetically. Check out those eyes, Ivy said to herself. "But you have to understand how important these meetings have been. At least I have a chance to make it up to you, now that you know what was going on."

He placed his right hand on the armrest of her chair to steady himself. She couldn't resist placing her hand on his.

"I'm sorry, Ned. I misunderstood. I didn't realize. I—"

"It isn't your fault, Ivy. It was just circumstances conspiring against us. We can put that right. And I can show you how much I appreciate you."

He checked his watch.

"It's a quarter to five. What say we knock off early and go for a bite to eat? Do you have to be anywhere this evening? I know a smashing place by the cricket ground. You'll love it."

He stood up and reached for the phone.

"I've just remembered," said Ivy. "I haven't e-mailed my work in."

"Why not do it now?" he said as he dialled. "Let's see if the system works."

Ivy opened up her case, pulled out her laptop, and logged on.

"Is there a password for the Wi-Fi?" He rifled through some documents on his desk while waiting for the restaurant to answer and located his diary. He carefully opened the inside front cover and pointed to the handwritten code.

Ivy opened her e-mail account. There was an e-mail from Sylvia in her Inbox with an attachment she'd sent as a trial run. Ivy opened them both to verify that everything was working then sent her Word document to Sylvia's account. At the same time, the virus that had been hidden in the attachment to Sylvia's e-mail replicated itself and sent copies to everyone in Ivy's address book, including the Queen Elizabeth Hospital, the Children's Hospital, and half a dozen charities. This was a new and especially nasty virus, Yardbird, able to circumvent all known firewalls and capable of reproducing itself so efficiently that within hours it had crashed the hospitals' mainframes and, thanks to its malicious program, erased the files of millions of patients in addition to the software running CAT scanners and MRI, dialysis, and X- and Gamma-Ray machines in departments around the country. It's always difficult to be precise in these matters to determine the damage caused, not least because there are always delayed, invisible, latent effects, not just on patients but on the bereaved, too, so it would not be fair to assign a precise number of deaths or injuries to Ivy's actions in sending that one e-mail; suffice to say that over the next twelve months western Europe saw a rise in its mortality rates not encountered since the Second World War.

"It works," said Ivy.

Ned smiled and booked them a table to celebrate.

Chapter Twenty-one

Fourteen times did she take the fox across the river, but the health of the chicken improvèd not.
 St. Tatrius's Sermon to the Flatworms 3:10

She could tell Ned was impressed. What had begun as an uncomprehending look of confusion quickly became one of shock and was accompanied by a sharp gasp as it transformed into a vacant, transfixed, transcendent gaze of ecstasy, as Ivy's fingers got to work. He didn't know if she'd been practicing or if she'd been holding back on their previous night together, and the truth was he didn't care one jot, but the relationship was taking on a whole new complexion, and Ivy herself was acquiring new qualities that Ned would never have dreamed of ascribing to her.

"Are you busy this afternoon?" he asked her the next morning over breakfast in bed. Ivy knew straightaway that Siobhan's advice had paid off. He wanted to see more of her.

"I had no major plans. Maybe go shopping." It wouldn't have surprised her if he'd said he wanted to spend the rest of the day in bed.

"Oh. Only it's the Donkey Derby in Shirley Park. Do you fancy going?"

"You're pulling my leg."

She bit into a slice of toast, lightly buttered.

"Not at all. I know it sounds a bit naff, Ivy, but the church, the old man, is sponsoring one of the races. They have a hospitality tent set up there ... actually, it's for recruitment purposes, but there's a private members' area where we can have strawberries and cream and champagne and stuff. It'll be fun."

"I don't know ..."

"Round up some of your friends. Sam. Anyone you think might enjoy it. I promise you it'll be a laugh, Ivy." He kissed her playfully on the lips and nibbled her ear.

"Okay, okay. I'll ask Sam and his Nana. I'm sure you're right. There's nothing I can think of more low-brow, but they can treat it with a knowing irony and pretend they're not actually enjoying it."

"Good."

"Does this involve gambling? I'd have thought the church was opposed to that sort of thing."

He squeezed her thigh.

"We don't like to call it gambling. It's called 'divinely ordained providence assessment.' But yes, you can have a flutter if you want."

"Excellent. I know Nana will love that."

―――

She nipped home to change and phoned Sam. He didn't sound too keen when she explained Ned's involvement in the Donkey Derby, but Nana overheard the conversation and let him know with little ceremony that she'd already planned on attending anyway, and when she learned after taking the receiver from him that she'd have somewhere to sit in the shade while being waited on, there was nothing Sam could do to dissuade her or to stop her from roping Caroline into the day out.

There were hundreds of people milling around at the entrance to Shirley Park when Ivy, Sam, Caroline, and Nana arrived. The Donkey Derby had long been a fixture on the Shirley social calendar, and for anyone who was anyone or who wanted to be a someone in Shirley, attendance was mandatory. The Rotary Club had been running the event for nigh on forty years, certainly for as long as Ivy could remember—she'd gone every year as a girl—and from the moment the mayor declared the event open to the fireworks display that brought the day to a close, the well-heeled, notable, and best and brightest citizens of the town made it their business to be seen and acknowledged by their peers, their inferiors, and the fourth estate, i.e., two trainee journalists from the *Solihull News*.

No one was exempt from the 50p entrance fee, however, paid with good grace by all those already through the temporary turnstile ahead of Ivy and Sam. While they queued, Ivy watched melted ice creams held in sticky, undersized hands dribble unobserved by their owners onto the tarmac, as excitable, moist-faced kids chased one another around and between parents' legs or teased lapdogs being led along the side of the Saracen's Head pub and into the park proper. The high-pitched shrieking, the futile, exasperated barking, the jovial, unrestrained banter of hawkers of toffee apples and candy floss, and the roaring of traction engines swirled around them, a heady mixture that, in the heat, gave the day a lightness, a dreaminess that took Ivy back to a childhood Sunday afternoon in Bourton-on-the-Water when they'd visited the model village and she'd felt faint in the sunshine and had to be revived by tea and scones with strawberry jam and clotted cream, the first time she'd ever tasted them. She'd always believed that her recall of that day had been corrupted, that her memory had added that gauze-like soft focus retrospectively, yet here it was again; unless she was experiencing déjà vu and her brain was playing tricks on her, those halcyon days were here again.

The focus of the festivities was an oval racetrack surrounded by makeshift wooden barriers considered sufficient to separate participants from spectators. Parents were expected to be responsible enough to supervise their offspring while races were in progress, although when Ivy saw the donkeys, she thought the idea laughable that children might need protection from such harmless-looking creatures. When she was small, they'd seemed terrifying; she was small still, it was true, but now she had a greater appreciation of the relative dangers posed by donkeys and small children.

"I suppose we should try to find Ned and his crowd," she said after they'd treated themselves—Ivy and Sam to Vimto and ready salted crisps, Caroline to milk and peanuts, Nana to tea.

"I could do with a sit down, sweetness," said Nana, trailing behind them. "And we haven't had a look at the race card yet. We'll need time to peruse the form, and I'm sure we won't recognize the names of the trainers."

"Nana, it's only a bit of fun," Caroline chastised her. "The most you can bet is a pound." Nana raised the forefinger of advice.

"No excuse for ignorance when the information is available. I'm sure Ivy would be the first to remind you of the value of research."

Ivy nodded in agreement, though she wasn't really listening. Instead, she'd been scanning the park for the hospitality tents. They'd be close to the main path into the park, she'd assumed. These events were always organized to facilitate businesses. And there they were: a row of modest, white marquees lining the main straight of the course, where the finishing line had been perspicaciously located.

They had arrived in time for the first race, and the participants were still being paraded around the makeshift paddock, the riders mostly teenage girls or young women, the odd male rider looking embarrassed and hoping not to be spotted by his mates. Nana agreed to forgo a bet on the first race to expedite the search for the Hartfields' tent, but Caroline was dispatched to watch the race and take note of the finishing order so that Nana could compare the result with the formbook. The others made their way around the track to the tents, which were facing onto a tarmac path, the private enclosures behind them overlooking the track so that invited guests could observe events in relative luxury.

Small groups of reps in jackets and straw boaters were gathered in the gardens in front of the tents, a dozen in all, one or two of the more officious checking the passes of those wishing to enter. The Hartfield tent was half-way along; Ivy identified it thanks to the sight of Ned's father, head and shoulders above everyone else in the immediate vicinity, and by the sound of Ned's laughter, which carried all the way down the row and above the sounds of generators, clowns, and braying debs. She grabbed hold of Nana's hand, not to drag her along but, perhaps subconsciously, to compel Nana to think well of these people, as though she was reminding Nana of a debt.

Ned saw them approaching from one tent away.

"IVY! YOU'RE HERE!"

It was as though a fighter plane passing overhead had just broken the sound barrier. Ned's voice silenced everyone in the adjoining tents, and when they turned to locate the source of the noise, they'd naturally followed Ned's line of sight to Ivy, so that suddenly there were fifty or sixty strangers looking at her in complete silence, the sound of a Wurlitzer in the distance the only interference—that, and a slight summer breeze that had been there all the time but which she only now could hear.

The three of them walked in silence towards the gate of the Hartfield enclosure, and Ned met them there, kissing Ivy over the gate before opening it. Conversations elsewhere resumed, heads turned away, and minds recovered their previous focus as Ivy ushered Nana forward.

"Ned, this is Nana. She's Sam's grandmother. You know Sam. Nana, this is Ned."

Ned bowed excessively, smiled politely, and offered Nana his hand.

"A pleasure to meet you, Nana. Please, do come inside. You'll find it's much cooler in here, in the tent."

"Thank you, Ned. I've heard a great deal about you."

He eyed Ivy suspiciously.

"I trust it was accurate information and met with your approval."

"Accurate so far," she said, teasing him. "Ivy told me you were a large chap."

"You can tell, then, how diligent she is in her research," he joked. He was discreet enough to avoid any double entendres, Ivy observed.

"Do ... please ... come through."

He made a path for them through the cluster of transfixed listeners gathered around his father, who was holding forth on some nonreligious topic or other. It would have been impolitic to interrupt, Ivy realized, which was why Ned took them straight into the tent itself, not all that much cooler but provided with a number of Formica tables and a bar, behind which a wispish, eagle-eyed, beaver-toothed man in a bow tie poured out glasses of champagne and Buck's Fizz for dignitaries and guests.

Ivy recognized Ned's mother, who was talking to the mayor and his wife. She peered over the mayor's shoulder at Ivy, then at Nana and Sam, while the mayor spoke, then returned to the conversation without pause; Ivy saw that her eyes darted back to them from time to time. Probably trying to find the right moment to escape the mayor and say hello, she thought.

Ned sat them down and brought over glasses of champagne.

"Cheers. So glad you could all make it," he said, raising his glass.

"Ooh. That reminds me, Ned," said Ivy. "Sam's sister, Caroline, is out there somewhere. We'll have to keep an eye open for her. She's watching the first race."

"Of course. No problem. We can broadcast a message over the Tannoy if you want, tell her to come to Tent Seven."

"That'd embarrass the hell out of her," said Sam. "Yow must do it."

"I hope, by the way, you've kept your entrance tickets with you," said Ned, pulling up a chair next to Ivy. "You'll need them for the race we're sponsoring. We're holding a lottery."

"What do we win?" asked Ivy.

"You get a voucher for a meal at the Shirley Temple and, much more fun, you get to ride in the race. Have you ever been on a donkey, Ivy?"

She scratched her head with her free hand.

"When I was a little girl, I think. On holidays."

"Well you can have my ticket as well, Ivy," said Nana, putting her glass down on the table and fishing out the crumpled laundry ticket from her purse. "I've no wish to endure the indignity of being carried round Shirley Park in the presence of my peers."

"Hey, Ned," said Sam, the champagne having gone straight to his head. "I hope yow don't win. Yow'd kill any donkey yow sat on. It'd 'ave to ride on yowr back instead."

It was an image Ned didn't find that amusing.

"Indeed."

Ivy glanced outside, through the opening of the tent, and saw Caroline passing by. She'd missed them. Ivy put down her glass and rushed out, calling after Caroline, waving her back, and opening the gate to let her into the enclosure.

"I thought you'd be stood outside," she explained as Ivy brought her in.

"It's cooler in here. Would you like some champagne?"

"No thanks. I'm fine."

Ned was out of his seat in an instant, his hand already extended. And his tongue, too. And his eyes, those beautiful eyes, were aglow. Ivy had come to expect this sort of attitude from men, and it didn't diminish her fondness for Caroline, but she'd have preferred it if Ned hadn't been so blatant. It was in his nature, she knew, and she somehow had come to terms with his lack of embarrassment, his lack of self-consciousness—it was one of the advantages of money, Ivy had learned, that those who possessed it rarely had to think about others' opinions of them. A sort of wealth-induced Asperger's.

Ned did not just ignore the presence of other minds in the room. He seemed to be oblivious to their very existence. Nor did he seem conscious of the embarrassment he might have caused Caroline by ogling her, let alone the embarrassment he was causing Ivy. If he wanted something, he simply said so.

"Jesus Christ!" he exclaimed, forgetting the inappropriateness of such an ejaculation. "Aren't you just the most gorgeous thing to walk through that door today? I must be having a vision!"

Ivy coughed. He should have said that to *her*.

"I'm Ned. Ned Hartfield. It's an absolute pleasure to meet you."

He was pumping Caroline's hand ferociously. Despite the violence of the greeting, she remained calm and unperturbed, weighing him up coolly.

"Ned, this is Caroline. Sam's sister."

Ned's manual convulsions stopped abruptly, but he kept her hand in his.

"*Sam* Sam? *Your* Sam? *This* Sam?" Ivy nodded.

"My goodness. What happened there then?"

Ivy didn't catch Ned's drift, but Caroline did and immediately took offence; she was naturally protective of her brother, and it was a question she'd heard before.

"Sam," she said, before Ned could expostulate further, "Let's go and put a bet on the second race. Nana, have you had a chance to pick something?"

"I haven't sweetheart. Just put me a pound on Number 5, would you? It was always my lucky number."

"Will do."

Caroline disengaged her hand from Ned's and nodded at him out of politeness, no smile warranted, even though Ned's gaze had never left her. She strode for the door, Sam in her wake, he too having failed to grasp what had transpired. Ned sat back down.

"Well," he said. "What a babe. I tell you, Ivy, Sam's a very lucky boy."

Nana had been keeping her head down, studying the race card, but she'd been taking in the conversation, and this was a bit much.

"In what way, Ned, would you say he is? Lucky, I mean."

Ned was unabashed.

"Of course, Nana, I know he's her brother, but you only have to look at her … Can I ask you … do they have the same parents? I only ask because, well, she's so stunning and Sam is …" He tried to find an adequate description of Sam. "… not."

"Excuse me?" Impertinence was an accusation that had never been levelled at Ned before. He assumed that Nana's confusion arose from a lack of clarity, not from too much.

"I mean he's so scrawny, so greasy, so … I've seen scabs more appealing, Nana, and that's a fact. It's only natural that people would wonder whether he and that vision of loveliness shared the same genes."

Nana willed herself not to be appalled. She was here as a guest, after all, and this young man was supposedly Ivy's beau; she didn't want to make a scene and upset Ivy. And the truth was that, had she been like most people, she would have lashed out wildly at Ned, in part because she was hurt by the thought that there might be some truth in what Ned was saying about Sam, her beloved Sam. She'd never loved him any the less for who he was, for his skinniness, his lack of worldly ambition, his bookishness. Her instinct was, like Caroline's, to defend his right to be himself. But she also knew that there was no need to justify her love for Sam, nor Sam himself, to this man. He was arrogant, headstrong, and condescending, and Ivy would learn that. Ivy would learn what was valuable. Eventually.

"Tell me, Ivy," Ned continued. "Does Caroline have a boyfriend? I'm sure she must. Probably a stockbroker or something."

Ivy shook her head.

"No. No. Caroline is a busy girl. She doesn't have a lot of time for that sort of thing."

She could almost hear the machinery at work in Ned's brain. He was fantasizing about what he'd do to Caroline. Ivy wanted to do something there and then, to slap him or stomp out, but she didn't want to leave Nana on her own, and Nana at least had somewhere to sit down while they were in the tent.

Instead, she took it out on the champagne.

By the time of the last race, she'd lost count of how many glasses she'd had. Sam and Caroline had been going back and forth, between the tent and the bookies, placing bets for Nana, who had remained in the tent with Ivy all afternoon; sometimes they returned with money, but mostly not.

The last race was sponsored by the Transcendental Gospel Crusade, and so everyone was driven from the tent to spectate. Or, indeed, participate, for the lottery was due to be drawn by George Hartfield, beyond the crowds now, in the middle of the track. Several hundred onlookers had gathered to see him, still aboard his Segway, which was itself on a raised platform, as he pulled the tickets from a revolving drum: kids were still running around, but there were a few tears now, time, fatigue, and excitement having made them fractious, and there were hundreds of flattened beer cans and plastic cups to provide a crispy underfoot. Ivy, Nana, Caroline, and Sam wandered across to join the assembled mass. Ned was standing at his father's side but saw them arrive and cast a grin in their general direction.

"Grey ticket, two hundred and thirty-four," George announced over the speaker system, and everyone bowed their heads, as though in prayer, to check their tickets.

It was Ivy's. Of course it was.

Sam spotted it first. All the champagne had taken its toll on Ivy's capacity to focus, although she'd been trying vaguely to study Ned's behaviour, to see how frequently he checked out Caroline.

"That's yow, Vee. Hold it up." He grabbed her arm and raised it above her head. "Over here, mate. Here she is." And Caroline said to Nana, "It must be fixed."

Ivy smiled inanely at all the fuss, knowing that she'd won something but having forgotten what was involved. By the time she reached the platform, the fresh air had rendered her giggly and flirty, so much so that the prospect of donkey racing seemed like a hoot. She sidled up to Ned and smiled blissfully at him, no longer perturbed by his fascination with Caroline. He took her hand and squeezed it. She knew it meant he loved her.

After the other five numbers had been called, the riders—Ivy, four children, and a teenage boy forced to endure the humiliation of having his parents watch—were kitted out with helmets and knee pads, then led to the paddock to select their charges. As the first number to be drawn, Ivy had the first choice. Ned, who had accompanied her and who knew about these things, sidled up to her.

"Number 1, Vee. I've got inside information. It's the shortest race of the day and that one has great acceleration."

"Yes," she agreed, looking at Number 2. "And it has eyes like Bambi." Her vision blurred and she looked back to Ned for confirmation.

"I don't think that will help you win, Ivy, but it's an observation I'm sure that has significance for you. Let me help you on."

He held her hand as he guided her to the palest and most sinewy of the six beasts (not the one with eyes like Bambi, but Ivy didn't realize), and lifted her on board, without objection from rider or donkey.

"There. Now, Lily will lead you to the starting line. Just you hold tight."

"Is that her name? Lily?" said Ivy, stroking the animal's neck.

"No, dear. This is Lily." Ned indicated a small, cheerful, ruddy-faced, fat-armed lady who looked like she'd escaped from a Blackpool postcard. "She's the owner of your ride."

"Hello, Lily," said Ivy, a little disappointed. "What's his name?"

"Ned," said Lily.

"No, I know that. What's the donkey's name?"

"Yes, dear. It's Ned."

Which would have been an unending source of merriment for Ivy had the race not intervened.

Intervened because, although Ivy was highly inebriated and giddy enough, she soon found to her amusement, then to her pleasure, and then to her delight, that the gentle jogging of the animals as they were led out to the race was the cause of some friction between her legs that could only be described as arousing. Thus, her amusement at the thought that her lover shared the same name as her donkey was somewhat overpowered by the insistent throbbing of her rapidly engorging clitoris. Had she been more circumspect, Ivy might have reflected on the irony of the sexual stimulation she was deriving from another Ned, another ride, as the Irish say, but such was the excitement and the level of alcohol in her bloodstream that she missed that particular opportunity for symbolism.

As the race began and the crescendo of noise drowned out particular conversations, Nana found herself next to a gaunt, pinched-faced woman she had seen earlier in the day; in the same tent, in fact, where she'd spent the afternoon. She cast a cautious eye over Nana, having felt unable to introduce herself before now, but as the crowd grew noisier and more distracted, she felt able to make Nana's acquaintance.

"We didn't meet earlier. I'm Ned's mother. Valerie."

"Pleased to meet you, Valerie. Amanjeet."

"Anjeet?" She frowned. She couldn't quite hear properly and it was a strange name.

"Amanjeet."

"Lovely. Are you related to Ivy?"

Nana shook her head.

"Ivy's friends. Sam and Caroline."

Valerie nodded to signify her familiarity. She had seen them earlier.

"What are you doing here?"

It was a strange question. What did she mean?

"I think Ned requested that Ivy bring some friends." She shrugged her shoulders. Had she done something wrong?

"No. I meant in Solihull. You aren't exactly a typical resident."

"I don't follow you," Nana said, although she suspected she did, and when Valerie replied, not by saying anything but by looking Nana up and down, at her clothes, she understood only too well. And she understood then why Ned had ushered her inside the tent when they'd all arrived.

She would not rise to the bait. Instead, she played Valerie at her own game.

"My husband was white, Mrs. Hartfield. That must have been how I gained access to Solihull. Of course, he never let me leave the house during the day in case anybody saw me, but it was a small price to pay to live in an area of such respectability ... such ... class."

Incredibly, her answer seemed perfectly reasonable to Valerie, who recognized no sarcasm in Nana's voice, even in the way she'd spat out the last word.

"Was your husband from Solihull originally?"

Could she *be* more offensive? Would no true Silhillian stoop so low as to marry an Asian?

"He was from Scotland, Valerie. From Glasgow." And then, mischievously. "Do you know it?"

It was a rhetorical question. Valerie knew *of* it, no doubt, but nothing more than that it was a place of no consequence. Her nod was in response not to Nana's question but in confirmation to herself of her own suspicions, an "I thought as much" upon hearing the negative response to her own inquiry. There was no further attempt at intimacy, no notice taken that Nana had used the past tense to refer to her husband, not even an effort to bring the conversation to a close with felicitations or solicitations. The conversation, Valerie had decided, was at an end. She had Nana's number. And Nana had hers.

Further conversation was redundant, but also impossible, as it happened, for the race was coming to a climax, as was Ivy. As the competitors rounded the last bend, Ivy was being jiggled and juggled by her steed, her face not just flushed but crimson, her features contorted as though in pain, but in fact expressing quite the opposite sensation, her body writhing under barely containable pressure, her heart pounding with every stride, and anyone within earshot, had they been able to isolate her voice, would have heard her moans of ecstasy as she called out in exasperated, drawn-out gasps, "N-N-N-e-d-d-d … N-N-N-e-d-d-d-d-d."

As she crossed the finishing line ahead of her rivals, a roar of elation erupted from the crowd, a cascade of lights exploded in Ivy's head, heat coursed through every vein in her body, and hats, flags, and fireworks rocketed skyward. No one had ever seen a rider give so much to win a prize so small. Enthusiastic spectators massed around the exhausted winner, patting her on the back, the only part of her body they could reach since Ivy was now slumped against Ned's neck, on the verge of sleep. Lily came among them to reclaim her property, and the crowd parted as one as she took Ivy and Ned through to the winner's enclosure.

Chapter Twenty-two

I know, I have known, I will have known
                                            Tenses 9:222

Ivy had never slept as soundly as she did the night of the Donkey Derby. It was with the best of intentions that she'd tried to stay awake that evening at Nana's, but the mixture of champagne, fresh air, sunshine, and postorgasmic languor had put paid to any thought she might have had of beating Sam at Shipmate, the intergalactic piracy game, even though they let her be Buccaneer Rogers and Sam was only Dockhand Dick. Sam had strolled it, his job made easier by Ivy's early departure for bed, ably assisted by Caroline, otherwise known as Slickleg Sally. And Nana, playing Captain Quelch, put up only a feeble resistance to Dockhand Dick's nefarious deeds, largely because her mind was on other things.

Much of Nana's evening was spent sipping parsnip wine and studying Sam contemplatively or looking absentmindedly into space as she reflected upon what she'd learned that day about Ivy's suitor and his family, and as she dealt with her own annoyance at the negative statements she'd heard expressed about her grandson. She was trying to bring herself to the necessary resolution: to decide whether to disregard the criticisms, continue to love and cherish Sam the way she always had, and let him and Ivy make their own way in life, learn its harsh lessons from bitter personal experience, discover for themselves some unwanted truths about human nature, and be forced into making unpleasant life- and friendship-changing decisions; or to intervene, act so as to protect them from possibly unnecessary harm, warn them, guide them, offer them assistance in some form other than standing back and allowing them to lose their sensitivity and develop some independence.

She was beginning to feel like Hamlet.

There was no reason why racism should be tolerated, she concluded. People like that had to be resisted. Why let poor Ivy fall into the hands of such prejudice?

She cast a final look at Sam before she retired for the evening. Crouched there over the Shipmate board, his pointy elbows resting on bony knees, his hair shiny and unkempt, his shirttail hanging out, one sleeve rolled up, one down, and his black plastic digital watch—that would have to be the first thing to go. That and his power slouch.

There was plenty to be done, she decided. In Sam's case, she'd have to draw up a list.

―――

"Is it me," said Ivy as Sam pulled a wide-mouthed black plastic bottle from among the bushes, "or is the challenge going out of geocaching?"

They'd barely had a chance to stretch their legs or take in any Sunday-morning air. Sam had to confess to himself that he'd been underwhelmed when he checked the e-mail he'd received that morning and calculated that the location of the newest cache was barely three-quarters of a mile from home. He'd ridden there slowly and gone the long way—down Prospect Lane and almost the entire length of Ralph Road—to get to The Gulley, as it was universally referred to in these parts, a pedestrian shortcut that brought shoppers into the midst of Shirley's boutiques, supermarkets, and other suburban facilities lining that particular strip of the Stratford Road. They were nearly back at the park again, the site of Ivy's triumph the day before, though her mind that morning dwelt upon it but cursorily. They'd had to scour all the bushes and trees along The Gulley before locating the cache—to that extent, the challenge had remained—but since they'd set out, Ivy had been wondering only what the next counter would be. She was starting to amass a collection.

"It's our friend again," said Sam. "I suppose he must live around here too."

"You must admit it makes the whole thing very convenient for us, doesn't it?"

"Ahr. I wouldn't mind a longer ride though, to be honest." Ivy couldn't bring herself to agree. She always felt vulnerable on the back of the Durköpp, and holding Sam tighter only reminded her how insubstantial he was.

He was kneeling and turning the bottle upside down to empty its contents onto the tarmac. They scattered like voodoo bones.

"I suppose it's obvious what the choice has to be," said Sam, surveying the options he'd spread between them: a couple of retractable pencils that Sam wouldn't have minded, a miniature submarine with an air tube attached so you could make it dive or surface, a day-glo-pink Gonk, and a keyring mascot in the shape of an American football helmet—the Washington Redskins.

"Not very PC," Sam observed, "but you don't want that anyway, do you?"

No. She wanted the counter. And there it was, just like the other two. But this time, when they saw the image on the coin, they were lost for words. They looked at each other in muted confusion as they passed the counter back and forth between them. For there, clearly embossed and unambiguous, was what they both knew was the head of a donkey.

Caroline was stamping around upstairs when they arrived back at Nana's.

"Tae kwon do," was Sam's explanation. He considered that sufficient. It was enough to give Ivy a descriptive account of Caroline's endeavours, but no indication of the vigour of her efforts, the energy with which Caroline threw herself into her training, or the aggression she was exhibiting with regard to her imagined adversary. Nor as to who that adversary might be.

Nana was putting on the Sunday lunch. The mellifluous, savoury aroma of Sukhi Dal drifted through the house. Ivy's nostrils flared, her mouth filled with saliva.

"Do yow like that?" asked Sam. She was surprised he had to ask.

"It's gorgeous, Sam. Don't you?"

"Ahr. Are yow going to stay?"

"Can I?"

"Nana?"

"You're very welcome, sweetness. What's ours is yours, you know that … In fact …" She turned from the kitchen window to face the pair of them. "Why don't you stop every Sunday lunch, Ivy? It isn't any great hardship for me to increase the portions, and Sam will always lay the table, won't you, Sam?"

It was an instruction, not a question.

"Ahr. S'pose."

"Thank you, Nana. Thank you. It really does smell wonderful."

Sam hadn't taken the hint about laying the table. The three of them stood there waiting for something to happen. Eventually, Nana had to prompt him.

"You know where the cutlery is, Sam, don't you?"

"Oh. Ahr. Right."

He finally grasped that his new obligation began there and then, which was sufficient to initiate his delaying tactic.

"Nana, we wanted to ask you. What do you make of these?"

At his prompting, Ivy held out the three counters for Nana's inspection. She turned back towards the kitchen window, so she could see them in the light. Sam and Ivy moved to either side of her.

"They're like some sort of imaginary currency," suggested Ivy as Nana examined them, rubbed them, and rattled them against one another.

"They're too light to be genuine though," Sam interjected. "I thought they might be souvenir badges; like you used to get from petrol stations."

Nana nodded, understanding but not entirely agreeing. She took another look at the devices.

"It's possible, I suppose, but do you know what I think?"

"What?"

She handed them back to Ivy.

"I think they're tokens. You'll probably find you can exchange them for something."

"For what?" Sam said, unconvinced. "There isn't a brand name on them or anything."

"Maybe that's what the M is," said Ivy. "They all have that symbol on."

"Could be that's it," said Nana, trying to be encouraging. "I tell you who'll know for sure."

"Who?"

"Jack Pance."

It was as though Nana had flashed the pope. Daring. Unthinkable. Conducive to cardiac arrest.

"Mad Jack Pance?" said Sam, checking he'd heard correctly. Nana's eyes confirmed that he had indeed.

"Mad Jack Pance, the wise nutter of Palmers Rough?" said Ivy, ensuring they were talking about the same Mad Jack Pance.

"Mad Jack Pance, the wise nutter of Palmers Rough and Pus, his passive-aggressive dog?" said Sam one last time, just to see if the suggestion became any less scary the more frequently it was repeated.

"Yes," said Nana. "Do you know him?"

"Never heard of him," said Sam.

But everyone knows Mad Jack Pance, even if they deny it. What horrified Sam and Ivy was nothing more complicated than the prospect of being seen in public with him. No one associated with Jack and Pus. They were tolerated, but no more.

And yet, oddly, they were also held in awe, since it was true that Jack's madness was not a frenzied dementia but a peculiar, obtuse wisdom. Thus, the qualifying adjective to his nickname: The *wise* nutter.

"Pop down to the woods and ask him," Nana advised. "I'm told Pus doesn't bite these days. And he's too laconic to snarl."

"You're telling me," said Sam. "That dog even shits sarcastically."

"Sam!" Nana scolded. "True as that may be, I've got the lunch on. We don't need those sorts of images at this time of the day."

"Sorry, Nana."

"I think we ought to have a little talk about your tactlessness, don't you?"

"Yes, Nana."

About time, too, thought Ivy.

Chapter Twenty-three

Eat not of those beasts possessed of knees. Unclean in my sight are those whose bellies may touch the ground.
The Book of Natasha 6:66

They came on foot, which was probably for the best: Palmers Rough could do without further erosion by bikes. There has been woodland here since before the Domes Day Book was compiled, and because of the soil it's home to oak and birch as well as Mad Jack Pance. It also used to be part of the Forest of Arden, but sheep grazing and arable farming reduced its size, and now they've designated it a Local Nature Reserve in the hope of preserving what's left.

Sometimes it feels like an animal version of New Street Station, what with all the foxes, woodpeckers, voles, bats, owls, not to mention the gangs of bloody kids on mountain bikes squealing around the coppices and chain smoking crafty fags as part of their initiation into adolescent life. That and being dragged backward through the stingers. Not the place for a recluse seeking solitude and tranquillity, but you can't tell people that.

One of the principal misconceptions about Jack, you see, is that he's seeking solitude and tranquillity. They imagine that because he's undemonstrative, because he lives in a wooden shack in the glade of Palmers Coppice with no one for company but a labrador/sheepdog mongrel—albeit an especially prepossessing one—because he stares at the shoppers coming out of Tesco, he must be antisocial, must prefer the company of his own inner demons and torments. But that's not Jack at all.

No. Jack is where he is because of the danger he thinks he poses. Because he so loves people that he struggles not to warn them of the impending apocalypse. He understands that humans are fragile, delicate, vulnerable beings, building their beliefs, their self-esteem, their self-justifications on the flimsiest of foundations, and the temptation to confront them with the futility of their architectural pretensions drives him wild; so wild that he would rather reduce his contact with them, regardless of how much it hurts him not to be among them. His compassion is deeper, stronger, more comprehensive than that of any man I've known, but he wrestles daily with the thought that if he really loved humanity he'd reach out to them and spell it out: that happiness is not enough.

There was still a sheen of dew across the glade when they arrived, a plane of crystal glistening in the sunlight. A miasma of smoke swayed upwards from the shack's chimney into the cloudless midsummer sky.

Ivy hesitated at the door before knocking. Mad Jack had a reputation for being unpredictable, an oxymoron of sorts, she realized, because reputations depend upon one's acting according to type. What she didn't know was what form his unpredictability would take.

"Come." She had no more time to ponder this paradox. Somehow, Jack had divined that he had visitors.

Ivy Feckett is Looking for Love

His door is never locked. People can wander in whenever they please, although most of them have the decency and sense of etiquette, like Ivy and Sam, to knock or at least announce their presence, one way or another.

Ivy pushed open the door, expecting a creak and to find a straw-covered mud floor, so she was pleasantly surprised to see instead stripped pine flooring, Art Deco lighting, and a welcoming wood-burning stove. And the far wall was lined with books. It was the sort of place she'd have chosen for herself, only not in the woods, which gave her the willies.

I was lying in front of the stove, the warmest part of the shack. I raised my head to inspect the visitors and arched an eyebrow, but nothing more. I didn't want to seem impressed. You need to understand that although I'm what is known as an omniscient narrator, it doesn't follow that I know everything that is *yet* to happen, and thus my apparent indifference was less the result of a certain nonchalance in the face of foreseen resolution and more to do with having a reputation of my own to uphold, namely, one of world-weary disdain and disregard for the fumblings and machinations of the human race.

It isn't true that I shit sarcastically, by the way. I shit the same way everyone else does. I just don't wipe my arse. I'm a dog for God's sake.

At the far side of the dining table, Jack was poring over Suetonius's *Twelve Caesars*. He'd read it half a dozen times already but was always ready to return to it when attempting to descry the motives of some public personage or other. His half-moon glasses sat precariously on the tip of his nose, and to add to the surreality of the image presented to Ivy and Sam, he was wearing his toga. Well, I say toga; in reality, it's just a long shawl that he wears around the house when he can't be bothered to put underwear on. More like a djellaba, really. Anyway, he feels comfortable in it and it means I don't have to look at his bollocks. Sensibly, he adopts more traditional attire when mingling with the local populace, but here, in his own home, he feels quite entitled to dress as he pleases.

I was naked.

Jack looked up over his glasses at his guests like they were new arrivals at a particularly eccentric boarding school. He returned his attention briefly to his book to remind himself of the page number, then closed it, saying, without looking up,

"Sam MacPherson. *Kiddha?*"

Sam was taken aback at being spoken to in Punjabi. Jack's voice was heavy, dry, and gravelly, like he'd smoked sixty Woodbine a day since the age of three, but his pronunciation was precise, deliberate. Like a scholarly farmer or tubercular professor.

"Oh ... er ... *Kiddha.*"

"And this lady is?"

"Er ... Ivy ... Ivy Feckett. She's a friend of mine. A good friend. And Nana's. A friend of Nana's."

Jack bent forward across the table and extended a small, bony hand. Ivy stepped forward, courageously and confidently, so she imagined, and shook it. His handshake was gentle but also, she thought, measured, and measuring, as though Jack was capable of gauging her by the briefest of touches. He had communicated the extent of his experience, the limitlessness of his sagacity, in one action; he had told her there was so much she did not know.

"Amanjeet is a most astute and discerning lady. I trust her judgement almost as much as my own," he said, releasing her hand and indicating that they should sit in the plain wooden chairs before them.

"Of course," he went on, "Pus here doesn't have the same high regard for her as I do, but then one could generalize from that to his attitudes towards all people. If that's his attitude to her, imagine what he thinks of you."

They both looked down their noses at me warily. I pretended I didn't know I was being talked about and continued to gaze into the flames of the stove. Jack was just making a point of reinforcing my status as misanthrope.

"Now." He pushed Suetonius to one side. "What is it that you think I can help you with?"

Sam shifted in his seat to look at Ivy and nodded. She dug deep into her trouser pocket, lifting her backside off the chair to locate the tokens.

"We thought you might be able to help us identify these, Mr. Pance," she said and spread out the tokens with her fingers on the table in front of him.

Jack blanched. He pulled his chair away from the table, as if in revulsion.

"Where did you get these?" His tone was even, but there was a sense of exigency about the question that both Sam and Ivy could detect.

"Geocaching," said Sam.

"And this Joe Cashing. Is he a friend of yours?"

"No," said Sam. "Geocaching. We go geocaching on my Durköpp every Sunday. I look for clues to caches online then use a map and my GPS unit to locate them."

Jack turned to Ivy.

"What language is this he speaks? Joe Cashing. Der kupp. Jeepee-yes. I know not these words."

Ivy was conciliatory. "He has his own language, Mr. Pance. He is not of this world."

Sam was beyond responding to sarcasm.

"Do yow know what they are, Jack? I thought they might be petrol station souvenirs. Yow know, like world cup team badges or something."

Jack had already risen from his chair and began to pace the floor. Even I was startled but pretended to be asleep.

"Do you only have these three?"

They both nodded.

"Then it has begun."

"Are there more?" The completist in Sam was awakened. "We're going caching again this Sunday—they've been turning up every week. How many more can we expect?"

Jack returned to the table and rested on his fists.

"There are only four. But you must promise me, if you find the fourth, that you will return here straightaway. And tell no one of your discovery."

Now Sam was intrigued.

"Yow said 'It has begun.' What has begun, Jack? Is it a competition? I thought it might be a treasure hunt, y'know, like in those rubbish novels back in the nineties. I thought we might've stumbled across some new version by accident."

"There is no treasure in this," Jack warned, the folds in his face closing up. Ivy was beginning to feel a tad unwelcome. Here was the predicted unpredictability. She got up to go, but she could tell Sam was eager to know more. She put a hand under one of his armpits, without thinking, to pull him up from his chair.

This was something she would never have dreamed of doing given a moment's circumspection. Sam's armpits had always been terra incognita to her, a fetid marshland of salty moisture, hot, uninviting, like sticking your hand in a bowl of hot caterpillars. On any other occasion, she would not just have recoiled: she would have hurled. Yet, to her surprise, there was no wetness, no pong, no sliminess. Sam was dry under his arms. Dry and clean. No sweat. It was weird. It was the weirdest surprise in an especially weird day. She pulled him from his seat and found herself inspecting her own hand and even, albeit tentatively at first, sniffing her own fingers. Nothing. No odour at all. How thoroughly disconcerting. Nothing Jack Pance could do would match that.

And Mad Jack Pance was watching. Ivy realized that if she thought Sam's newfound hygiene was weird, imagine how she looked to Jack, standing there sniffing her fingers in the middle of his shack. She suddenly remembered shame.

173

"We have to go now, Sam. We've taken up enough of Mr. Pance's time."

"But we still don't know what they are," Sam protested. "Jack seems to know, don't yow, Jack?"

Jack said nothing. He just stood and stared. I thought it opportune to bark. Ivy got the message.

"Let's go, Sam." She dared to pull on his arm. Sam yielded.

"We'll come back if we get the fourth one," Sam promised. "Will yow tell us then?"

But Jack wasn't very garrulous. He just shifted his gaze to the door, a slight movement that Sam took to be a yes. It was good enough. Sam nodded in return and followed Ivy out of the room. I barked again.

"Yes, Pus, I know," said Jack. "So much knowledge. So little wisdom."

Chapter Twenty-four

And Reagan begat Saddam, and Bush begat Saddam, and Saddam begat war, and Bush begat war, and Bush begat Osama, and Osama begat war, and Bush begat Bush, and Bush begat war, and war begat war.
Hypocrites 9:11

When they weren't working, Sam and Ivy spent what time they had speculating about the meaning of the tokens and Mad Jack Pance's reaction upon seeing them. They went online and checked reference sites, numismatist sites, antiques and collectibles sites, anything they could think of that might yield a clue, and Sam kept a constant eye on the geocaching sites for any sign of a new cache being planted in the South Birmingham area. By the middle of the week, though, they were still no better informed.

Consequently, the train trip into work on Thursday morning was spent in silence, which is to say that Ivy and Sam were silent, even if their carriage mates were engaged in discussing items of varying degrees of triviality and at volumes in no way proportional. Ivy was, in any case, doing her best to blot out her surroundings: Only the night before, she had uploaded the new Kronos Quartet CD onto her smartphone and was giving it a try-out as a working-day mood setter while she edited the sum total of her week's research up to that point. Sam, who usually made his own way into the library, had phoned Ivy first thing that morning and asked if he could accompany her into town, explaining that he was taking the train for the remainder of the week while the Durköpp went in for a service. Ivy's suspicions had not been aroused, nor had she inquired as to the health of Sam's scooter upon encountering him at Solihull Station, having given no thought to how he'd made it there from home.

It was only because Sam had chosen not to dull his sensitivity to his immediate environment that he noticed the change in the atmosphere. He and Ivy had been lucky to get seats when the train pulled into the platform, squeezing in ahead of the pack and snapping up places right by the door, and the usual tactic upon the successful acquisition of a seat was usually to hide one's face in a book or turn up the music, but Sam, who had had the foresight to bring reading matter along with him, was nonetheless no seasoned traveller, and thus he was susceptible to the distractions that presented themselves at each lurch and sway and opening and closing of the doors.

Whereas they had boarded a boisterous carriage of commuters already anticipating the weekend and its concomitant frivolities, by Olton Station it was apparent that an air of sombreness had descended upon those commuters confined to the corner behind Ivy, although, further down the carriage, conversation was as lively and cheerful as before. Sam tried his best to immerse himself in his reading, while simultaneously ensuring that no one could peer over his shoulder and identify the text under scrutiny;

if asked about it, he had prepared the explanation that his grandmother had decided it propitious for him to familiarize himself with the culture and history of his ancestors. Ancient Indian works such as the *Mahabharata* and the *Ramayana* would inevitably be included in this curriculum, and it was only by the merest chance that he happened to be perusing the *Kama Sutra* at this moment. That someone might wonder what kind of grandmother would recommend as reading matter for her offspring's offspring a text widely regarded as a sex manual did not occur to Sam, precisely because Nana was exactly the sort of grandmother who *would* do that. Other folk might have raised an eyebrow—or two—upon getting such advice from their gran; Sam's concern was only that he not be spotted in public having done so. More tellingly, he didn't want Ivy to catch him without a plausible excuse.

At Acocks Green, two passengers stumbled out of the door onto the platform and vomited freely and at length. Before Tyseley, three more had turned paler than the page you're reading, and at Small Heath a six-foot-four-inch, 15-stone bodybuilder training at the College of Surgeons passed out on the floor of the carriage and had to be lifted out into the fresh air before other commuters could board. Of those who did board, taking the bodybuilder's place, one vomited, one fainted, and one woke up in a pool of vomit.

All of them had been reading over Ivy's shoulder.

Ivy, meanwhile, had decided that the new Kronos Quartet album was especially conducive to the production of a tranquil state of mind prior to a day of hard work. But as the CD came to an end, she raised her head from the text she'd been editing to see Sam motioning to her that she should remove her earphones.

"What is it?" She pulled one earphone out.

"What are yow reading, Vee?"

"Eh?"

"What are yow reading?"

She handed across her slab of A4.

"This week's research. Survivors' accounts of the genocide in Rwanda. I'm having to double-check the grammar and punctuation. Some of the pieces are just verbatim testimonies and I have to tidy them up."

Sam skimmed the top page and flicked over a couple more just to get a sample.

"Hey. Don't lose my place. I'm almost finished. It'll mean an easy day tomorrow."

He handed the slab back.

"Yow do realize, Vee, the damage yow could be doing by letting people see that?"

"In what way?" She was offended at the suggestion. "It's important that people know what happened there."

"Ahr, I agree. But that's not what I mean."

"What then?"

He thrust his head forward to meet her half-way and whispered.

"Haven't yow noticed the smell in here?"

Ivy arched her back and sniffed the air. The window above their seats was wide open, and gusts blew in intermittently so that there was only the gentlest hint of puke on the air.

"Something sweet and pungent," she said. "But faint. We've been through Tyseley."

She was pleased with her deduction and Sam didn't contradict her. People *did* need to know what happened in Rwanda, even if it made them sick. They just deserved a trigger warning, he felt, an opportunity to prepare themselves beforehand, and not be presented with the details unexpectedly. On the morning trip into work, for instance.

Ivy was still sniffing the air, though. She had picked up something else. A clean, slightly disinfectanty odour; something cosmetic but also grassy, rural. Her head made a series of small jerks as she tried to locate the precise source, to catch the trail of the scent. Suddenly, the breeze coming through the open window subsided, and she was able to trace it to its source. It was Sam.

"What have you got on, Sam?"

His cheeks turned pink. Ivy had never seen that before.

"Er ... Dolce & Gabbana ... pour Homme." It didn't sound so exotic when said with a Brummie accent, even if he'd said it with the quietest whisper he could manage, a breathless, almost erotic gasp, and Ivy's first instinct was still to say "You girl," but then she noticed something else.

"Sam ... you've had your hair cut."

Indeed he had. He'd had it cut two days before, in fact, but she hadn't noticed until now. That was how long it was since she'd last taken even a perfunctory, superficial glance at her closest friend, and it had all been down to the hint of puke on the wind.

"It suits you, Sam. Really."

She was compensating for her feelings of guilt at not noticing earlier, but at the same time she also felt decidedly odd. The world was not as it was supposed to be. She was looking at Sam in a new light. The smart, tidy, clean, sleek black hair. The youthful, zesty, lively smell. The embarrassed flushing of his cheeks.

Good grief, thought Ivy to herself. He's a handsome young man.

Chapter Twenty-five

Ask not why the ground doth shake with wrath at thy late rising. Ask rather why thou doest shake and the earth stand still.

The Book of Doreen 4:4

Ivy had neither seen nor heard hide nor hair of Ned all week. There were times when she'd forgotten all about him, stopped wondering where he was. She understood that, as her boss, he was in a precarious position, had to avoid accusations of favouritism. Did that mean he had to cut her out of his life entirely, though? Did it mean he couldn't contact her—or she contact him—outside of office hours?

Apparently so, since he'd made no attempt to call her, and when she'd phoned his place, all she ever got was the answering machine. Yes, she had called a couple of times without leaving a message, just to hear his voice, but then she realized what a terrible cliché it was, how juvenile, and tried to abstain altogether after making one last call, the night before, Thursday, asking him to ring.

There had been no reply by Friday night. She sighed, she felt frustrated, she didn't know what to do. But she also resolved to be angry with him, regardless of her sentiments concerning the status of their relationship. It was churlish of him not to reply to her calls, not to get in touch at all. An unforgivable lack of courtesy. Never mind whether or not he wanted to further their intimacy; if he had wanted to end things, he should at least have had the decency to tell her. As it was, he was treating her like she didn't exist, like they'd never met.

Siobhan was on an overnight in Paris, so it was just Ivy and Maggie that evening, each getting ready for the weekend in her own particular way: Ivy looking forward to a nice hot bath, a glass or two of Chablis, and Bryn Terfel in the background while she read Martha Nussbaum (Ah, Bryn Terfel—now there was a man with a booming voice who knew what to do with it), Maggie dancing upstairs in her room to the Black Eyed Peas as she tarted herself up and swigged Stella in preparation for a night in the city, looking to cop off with a nice-looking bloke with manicured fingernails and a few bob. It wasn't until she saw Ivy in the kitchen in her dressing gown that Maggie thought to ask if she fancied coming out. By that point, it was clear what Ivy's plans were, so she felt safe in asking. Ivy would undoubtedly have cramped her style, they both knew that. Fortunately, Ivy wasn't in the mood for a night on the tear, let alone being anywhere close to contemplating the possibility of chatting a guy up, although the thought briefly went through her head that it would have taught Ned a lesson.

She was leaning over the bath when Maggie knocked on the door to tell her she was off, and she was easing herself into the bath when the front door shut. She was happy to be left alone, to have the time and space to think, to finally wonder what had happened to Ned, to wonder about the tokens and Jack Pance, and, most of all, to wonder what had happened to Sam. Within a matter of, what, a week or two, he'd undergone a radical makeover. Of course, he still had that adenoidal Birmingham whine—which would never disappear—but that didn't really matter; Ivy had always thought it was what someone said, not how they said it, that counted. Still, she couldn't help noticing that he'd become more considerate, more thoughtful, and, well, cleaner, smarter, more pleasant to be around. The old Sam had been funny, but in a laugh-at-him rather than laugh-with-him way, and even then only if he wasn't being repulsive.

Maybe he had a girlfriend on the scene he hadn't told her about.

Of course! It was so obvious. He was going out with someone but was too embarrassed to admit it! Why hadn't she realized earlier? What other possible explanation could there have been? No wonder he'd blushed on the train.

Ivy felt very pleased with herself at having made sense of Sam's enigmas, and she congratulated herself for her increasing sophistication. Her powers of deduction were improving dramatically. Ever since she'd got back into the sexual saddle, since she got the tips off Siobhan, she'd developed a greater worldliness, she concluded; she was becoming womanly. A wise woman. Like in medieval days. She'd have been burned as a witch.

She smiled with self-satisfaction and found, all of a sudden, that Bryn Terfel's powerful lungs were moving her in more than one way. Maybe it was the vibrations making the bath shudder. Whatever it was, his voice was giving her permission to enjoy the feeling of her own body. The room was becoming exceedingly steamy.

She began to fantasize, to imagine it was a man between her legs rather than her own hand. She closed her eyes, and, in an effort to strengthen the illusion, to make it more vivid, she attempted to add some character, some personality, to this abstract man. The problem was, no sooner did she try, than she found herself thinking of Sam, the new Sam, and the problem with that was that the new Sam was too tightly bound up with the old Sam, Sam her friend, Sam her workmate, Sam, practically her brother ... And it just didn't work. She couldn't feel that way about him. He didn't turn her on.

And then she couldn't shake him from her mind. Damn! Sam! He'd ruined it.

The illusion was shattered. She gritted her teeth in frustration. Bryn warbled on. She could still feel the vibrations. She could have persisted, she knew, but it would have meant thinking of someone else. Thinking of Ned. And there was no way she was going to give him the satisfaction, whether he knew it or not, of being her indispensable phantasm. No. She would as soon do without altogether.

She took Martha Nussbaum to bed. And soon she was asleep.

It was three in the morning when Maggie climbed the stairs, doing all she could—in her intoxicated state—to avoid waking Ivy. She needn't have worried. Ivy was well away. Besides, if anyone was to have a problem with waking up, it would be Maggie. Her headache the next day rivalled Charles the First's.

As per her usual routine, based on the girls' tacit understanding, Ivy got up early on Saturday to head out to the shops. She dressed, washed, made herself breakfast, all as quietly as the church mouse for which she'd been so frequently mistaken in the past. Before venturing out, she made a list of things she had to get, compiling alongside it a list of things to look out for—things she'd have liked to get—folded it into her duffle coat pocket, and was about to nip upstairs to the loo when she heard the toilet flush and the loo door open.

She was half-way up the stairs, trying to be discreet and to avoid attracting attention, but she couldn't help getting a glimpse of Maggie's catch from the night before, the latest guy in her life. He was a big guy. A broad, hairless back, hard, muscular calves, a pair of red boxer shorts covering a broad but tight butt, and, atop his head, a jet-black curly mop of hair, trimmed and shaped. The body pushing open Maggie's door was one she recognized.

Ivy broke out in a cold sweat.

"Ned?" He turned. His blue eyes, those beautiful blue eyes, flashed. They were all the confirmation she required.

"Ivy?" He couldn't help but boom. "What are you doing here?"

But she wasn't there anymore. She was already at the front door. She couldn't stay for an explanation, or to answer any questions. What need was there?

"I have to go out. Shopping," she said, fumbling with the keys. Ned had crossed the landing to the top of the stairs but had gone no further, feeling vulnerable in his boxers and realizing the futility of pursuit. But he called out anyway.

"Ivy! Come back! Come back!" His voice could be heard right down Broad Oaks Road. And needless to say, Maggie heard it too. She woke up when she heard the front door slam to discover that a hangover was only the start of her problems.

Chapter Twenty-six

For that which is without a soul cannot be insulted. Verily, I say unto thee that kicking chairs harms none but the kicker.

The Book of Pseudo-Bono 17:99

Ivy barely knew what she was doing. Upon rushing out of the house, she had grabbed her bike, and without any further plan, she had pedalled furiously down the road, her head filled with manic, extreme, deeply powerful but incoherent ideas and conjectures, as she tried to make sense not just of what she'd witnessed but also her feelings about it. Through that mess, that chaos, came the very reasonable, possibly even predictable, plan of making for Earlswood Lakes, premised on her recollection that it was where Sam went whenever he wanted time to himself. That she made it across the Stratford Road was a small miracle, given how confused she was, but she got as far as the cycle path before her introspection was brought to an abrupt halt by the crowds blocking her way.

To give Ivy some credit, she *had* noticed the two coaches parked at the start of the path, but they hadn't caused her to speculate about their presence. She was far too caught up in deciding what she was going to say to Ned on Monday morning when she handed in her notice. Because, let's make no bones about it, this was a revelation that had to mean the termination of any contract, any contact, between the two of them; that much, Ivy was sure about. So, when the path was blocked by a swathe of what were quite clearly Japanese tourists, who, upon hearing Ivy approach from behind, turned around en masse and began to incorporate her image into their collection of memorabilia via various forms of camera, Ivy met them open-mouthed and silently—it didn't help that she spoke no Japanese.

But these weren't ordinary Japanese tourists. There was something not quite right about them. What was it? Could it be that half of them appeared to have rainbow-dyed Afros? And the other half were wearing glam rock–style sunglasses, yellow flares, and tie-dye shirts? This was no Sony Corp. outing to Milton Keynes.

At any other time, Ivy's newly acquired deductive powers would have set to work immediately, but this time, she simply posed the questions and made no effort to secure an answer.

It looked for a while like a stand-off might ensue, Ivy astride her bicycle and going nowhere, the Japanese clicking away at an authentic provincial in her weekend attire and apparently struggling not to cry. However, the loss of impetus in the forward motion of the group was noticed by its guide, who, although some way away from Ivy, could see there was someone on the other side of his charges trying to get through. He said something in a quiet, informal way to a number of those in his immediate vicinity, who then moved aside to let him advance. By repeating the same action, he made rapid progress, and after a minute or so he was standing before her, a smartly dressed but shaggy-haired chap of 30, Ivy reckoned, maybe 35, seeing the wrinkles when he smiled.

"Hi there," he said with a trendy-teacher nonchalance. "I'm hoping you might be my salvation."

Ivy didn't have time for this. She had more important things to sort out. Before she could demur, however, he was up close, and Ivy could see then that he was embarrassed about something.

"I'm afraid we're a bit lost. I have these two coach-loads of Japanese ELO fans who haven't eaten since they got off the plane at four this morning. We seem to have lost our way and we're looking for somewhere to get food. You wouldn't know if there any shops or anything like that around here?"

Ivy scratched her head. ELO? English Light Opera?

"You're in the back of beyond here," she said. "There are some pubs if you carry on along the path, in Earlswood, but they won't be open for another couple of hours."

He nodded dejectedly.

"They probably wouldn't do sushi anyway."

"I don't think they do," said Ivy, sympathetically. "But you could go up to the Lakes and get fish there." It was meant as a joke, but his eyes lit up.

"Lakes? That'd be perfect. Raw fish. What sorts do they have?"

Ivy couldn't tell if he was being serious. She was still trying to get her head around the idea of Japanese ELO fans. She knew she should recognize the name.

"I can't tell you, but there are always lots of anglers there. I'm sure they'd be willing to sell you some of their catch." She eyed him suspiciously. Was he honestly going to offer his guests fish straight from the lake?

"Excellent. Thank you very much, er . . ."

"Ivy."

"Ivy. Thank you. We won't detain you further. I'm sorry to have obstructed your path."

"Not at all. Good luck."

He returned to his group and bade them part so that Ivy could proceed. It was still a good couple of miles to the Lakes, so they had quite a walk ahead of them, and Ivy wouldn't see them for another hour at least, but they waved her off cheerily, and she managed a painful smile.

Within moments of leaving their company, she'd already put them out of her mind. It insisted on thinking of Ned.

———

True to form, meanwhile, Ned had sprung into action. Straight after Ivy left, he had dressed and was off down the street after her, leaving Maggie confused and in pain. He couldn't possibly have caught up with Ivy, but he wasn't really chasing too hard. He just wanted to see in which direction she was going. Once he was sure that she was heading for the Lakes, he let her be. Instead, he made for the house of that friend of hers. Sam's.

He strolled over from Broad Oaks Road to St. Bernard's Road. There was no point in rushing, and it gave him the opportunity to formulate some kind of excuse. Well, not an excuse. What needed excusing, after all? To all appearances, this had been nothing more than an unfortunate coincidence. If Ivy had got the wrong end of the stick about what was going on between them, about their *supposed* "relationship," if she'd gotten too serious about what had been nothing more than two bouts of undistinguished hanky-panky between acquaintances, well, it was very sweet and all, but, sorry, it didn't obligate him to rectify matters. "Good thing that she saw me," he confided to himself.

It wasn't Sam who opened the door, however. To Ned's delight, it was Caroline. She was in her grey cotton tracksuit.

"I'm sorry to bother you. It's Caroline, isn't it?" He advanced and shook her hand. "Ned. Ned Hartfield. We met at the Donkey Derby." Caroline nodded noncommittally. The fact that she hadn't smiled didn't register with him.

"I was hoping to have a word with Sam, as it happens. I don't know if he's in. Ivy and I have had a bit of a … er … a misunderstanding. Is he around?"

Caroline shook her head, but Ned had piqued her curiosity, so she didn't amplify. She was hoping he would elaborate, knowing he'd find any excuse to extend their conversation.

"Ah … erm … It's a tad embarrassing, to be honest." He lowered his voice. "A little delicate." He was still telling the whole street, mind you, and for all its delicacy, he couldn't resist telling Caroline. Maybe, for some reason, he thought it would impress her, that she would share his opinion of Ivy.

Because he knew his opinion was always right and suspected that he and Caroline were animals of a similar stripe. She was better than the rest of them. Like he was.

"I'm afraid Ivy caught me pretty much *in flagrante delicto*, if you'll excuse the euphemism," he explained, feigning regret but clearly proud of himself. "Saw me taking a bite of forbidden fruit."

Caroline's lips pursed. Blood rushed to extremities as her fight or flight instinct took over. She recalled Nana's account of events in the Hartfields' tent. But still she managed to restrain herself.

Ned was enjoying his confession. It turned him on that he could talk dirty in front of this utter babe.

"I'll be honest: We were both drunk … the lady in question … I say 'lady' although she clearly wasn't one, if you catch my drift … but Ivy wouldn't stay to listen … wouldn't let me reason with her … I don't know why I bother sometimes. Of course, nothing ventured, nothing gained, I suppose. How is one going to find out if a bird's any good in the sack if one doesn't give her a go?"

This was the closest Ned ever got to philosophizing. This was as deep as he went. And in such relative depths, he'd failed to notice the stance Caroline had adopted. He was noticing her legs, of course, and her waist, and her breasts, but not their particular configuration.

"Don't get me wrong now. I can't imagine for one minute that you'd disappoint *any* man, Caroline. You're an absolute stunner. Not like Ivy. And I bet you know a few tricks, too. Not that *that* matters, of course. I mean …"

He stepped in, a little too confident in himself, his cupped right hand moving only in one direction. Caroline stepped back into the hallway to avoid his grope. *Unbelievable!* But Ned still didn't get the message. He tried again.

"Don't be shy. I bet you get wet the instant my fingers touch your t—"

He was perhaps lucky not to have had the opportunity to utter that final thought; it would only have meant a more thorough pounding. As it was, the moment Ned's tongue touched the back of his teeth to pronounce that "t" coincided with the moment that Caroline's right foot met forcibly with what Ned sometimes, playfully, referred to as his "oyster bag." Few are the occasions in history that a man has been kicked so sweetly, so accurately, and so cleanly in the goolies as Ned was that day, and, to use his own turn of phrase once more, one might think one would feel privileged to participate so centrally in such a historic moment. On this occasion, however, one was so overwhelmed by pain that one was unable to acknowledge the distinction. Instead, Ned found himself observing a white wall of light as he collapsed to the concrete like a sweaty lettuce. There was no sound. No smell. No taste. Just a sheet of white light. Pure white light and the agony of having his knackers rung like church bells.

That hurt.

Chapter Twenty-seven

The symptom of the thief is the lock on the door; of the outcast it is the lock on men's hearts.
                                                      Belgians 12:5

"Yow'll get haemorrhoids sitting there."

Not so long ago, that was precisely the sort of comment Sam would have made upon finding Ivy on a boulder at the edge of the lake. Honest, unflattering, inappropriate, the first thing that came into his head, something he'd heard a thousand times as received folkloric wisdom among Brummies. And artless. But Nana had decreed that Sam would have to change, that a lack of artifice, while endearing, would not do in a world of intrigue, two-facedness, and complexity. He probably shouldn't have crept up on Ivy the way he did—that was out of nervousness, not a desire to surprise her—an indication that he was still a work in progress, but everything else he did was right. He placed a gentle hand upon her shoulder and said in a comforting, reassuring tone,

"Caroline said yow might have come out here."

Ivy said nothing. She resisted the temptation to cry initially, but as Sam sat down beside her and she realized he knew what had happened, relief surged through her, exploded like a firecracker in her stomach. She threw her arms around him and wailed. And wailed. And wept.

"Yow deserve so much better, Vee," he said, responding to her hug in kind, stroking the back of her head while she buried her face in his neck.

"There's no need to feel foolish. Yow were taken advantage of, pure and simple."

It wasn't much consolation, but it was reassuring to be told it. She drew back from him to wipe her eyes.

"I should have known better, Sam. I feel such an idiot for being so trusting, so willing to commit so quickly. I wanted to be in love so much. I was ready to fall for the first man who looked at me. It doesn't happen often, you know."

He was lightly grasping her by the shoulders, and hearing her say this made him want to shake some sense into her, but he opted instead for verbal remonstrance.

"Are yow being deliberately stupid, Vee? Don't yow know how much Nana loves yow, how much Caroline loves yow …" His voice softened. "How much I love yow? Yow are cocooned in love. Swaddled in it. It surrounds yow like a bubble. Yow don't need to go anywhere to find love. It's right here. It's wherever yow are."

She let out a sharp breath of self-deprecating laughter through her tears. She'd never heard it before, and this wasn't how she expected to be told she was loved. She hadn't prepared for it very well, had she?

She hugged Sam again and said thank you. It was a great comfort for her to hear they'd all been so concerned. It didn't make her feel any less of an idiot, mind you, and it was even worse now that those who loved her *knew* she was an idiot. That was a simple fact she'd have to live with. She'd been an idiot, and now she had to stop.

There was one other thorny issue she'd been too polite to mention. It hadn't just been love she'd been looking for. There was sex. That had to be dealt with too. She needed a good rogering from time to time, and with the best will in the world, that was something Nana and Caroline couldn't provide. They couldn't make her feel sexy, couldn't make a man ache for her. And as for Sam … They had too much history. She knew him too well.

Perhaps it was a positive development, then, that he was beginning to become somewhat alien, a bit different, less obvious, less himself. He'd always been like an open book to her, but recently she'd seen a side to him that was unexpected. Novel. She laughed to herself: Open book, novel. Very witty.

She'd always felt comfortable around him, had never had to be on her guard, but that had been because she believed there was nothing he could do to surprise her. Now he was revealing qualities that made her see him in a new light. And she liked what she was seeing.

He was about to say let's go home when there appeared, on the far side of the lake, through the trees, a silent, shuffling, sore-footed crowd of multi-hued, camera-toting Japanese tourists, headed by the unfortunate trendy-teacher guide Ivy had spoken to an hour or so before. Sam managed to utter a 'what the—?' as the group fanned out and, one by one, approached the anglers dotted along the bank.

"Oh, they're with me," explained Ivy, explaining nothing. "They were lost and hungry, and I suggested they try the fishermen. Japanese ... raw fish ... d'you see?"

Sam opened his mouth to say something then stopped, like he'd thought better of it. Instead, he nodded, stood up from the boulder, and held out his hand to help her up.

"Shall we go? Nana'll have the kettle on."

Ivy gave no reply. She just smiled up at him and accepted his offer of a hand.

Walking off towards the road, Sam pushing Ivy's bike, they failed to notice Jack and me, lurking in the woods. We'd been there all the time, waiting to see what would happen. Our suspicions were confirmed.

We knew what Sam was about to say but didn't. He didn't say it because he knew it would have upset Ivy. He was learning. And it was okay, because Jack was there to remedy the situation. It was Jack, rather than Sam or Ivy, who sought out the guide and told him, *sotto voce*, that there hadn't been any fish in Earlswood Lakes for the last ten years. And when the guide expressed mystification at the presence of so many anglers, it was Jack who explained to him the subterfuges that men sometimes go through to have one morning a week of peace and quiet to themselves, a place and a time for reflection and contemplation. Bewildered though he was, and no less hungry for being enlightened, the guide could empathize with that, and whenever he thought about that day in the years to come, it filled him with optimism and charitableness to think that so many middle-aged Englishmen could prefer to engage in pure philosophy, in such a harmless activity as imitation fishing, than beer-swilling aggression or the received prejudices of the weekend tabloids.

There is some good to be found in everyone, he would say.

Chapter Twenty-eight

After 40 days amongst them did he squint, for most pale was their flesh, and bleachèd were their teeth. And the Lord caused to be sent down unto Hesketh cases of tobacco and coffee, saying, 'Bring them to know the pleasure it affordeth me that they might drink of this brew and smoke of this leaf. Abhorrèd in my eyes it is that whiteness and goodness be confused.'
1 & 2 Loggets 2:2–4

It was Ivy who suggested they go geocaching the next morning. Sam had been unwilling to raise the subject, figuring Ivy needed to be treated more considerately. He'd been dying to go, of course, having learned only the night before that a new cache had been secreted in Malvern Park, and because Mad Jack Pance had intimated that there was only one more of those counters to be found. So he was delighted when, that Saturday night, during a less pugnacious than usual game of Swizzo!, Ivy had inquired about the state of the Durköpp.

"Running better than ever, Vee. I don't know exactly what the mechanic did—he must have tuned it up, anyway—but there's no rumble at all. It's a smooth ride now ... like yow wouldn't imagine."

"Must have knocked some of the rough edges off it, sweetness," said Nana, sipping cauliflower wine and passing a knowing look across at Ivy. She didn't catch the allusion straightaway, but gradually it dawned on her that Nana was telling her she'd had something to do with the new-look Sam MacPherson.

Deservedly, then, it was Nana who won the game that night. She was running a partnership hospital and had been selling donated body parts to pharmaceutical companies by the lorryload so they could carry out tests of their drugs without having to use animals. The hospital made money out of it, no animals suffered as a result of the tests, the public got new drugs for obesity, and the only people who, arguably, lost out were sentimental organ donors who imagined their body parts or the body parts of their loved ones were being used for transplant purposes and not to generate funds for the hospital and profits for Big Pharma. But as Nana pointed out, it was too late to matter for the donors themselves.

Sam, Caroline, and Ivy stood no chance in the face of such unassailable logic chopping. In their hearts it all seemed so horribly wrong, yet their heads couldn't generate an objection that could overwhelm the perceived benefits. In moral terms, it made Sam's role as an avant-garde painter of murder scenes seem clumsy and uncomplicated, and Ivy, a trade-union leader campaigning for a toughening of the immigration laws and retention of Trident, just seemed prehistoric, although her heart wasn't in it at all, especially seeing as she owed so much to Nana, an immigrant and CND campaigner.

Caroline had already had her moral compasses tested that day, and in the real world, too. A pacifist Tae kwon do expert faced with sexual harassment from a racist poshboy. What was one meant to do?

Nana told her she'd passed with distinction.

———

It suited Ivy's mood that the Sunday morning got off to a gloriously shining bright new beginning. The ride on the back of Sam's Durköpp was everything he'd promised: smooth, calming, enjoyable. This time, it was a genuine shame that the journey was so short, only into Solihull, to Malvern Park. Down Streetsbrook Road, straight over the roundabout onto Homer Road—uncomfortably close to the Hartfields' residence, Sam realized belatedly—up Church Hill Road to St. Alphege's Church. Rather than take Park Road, he continued up New Road. Ivy realized this was the longer way, but she guessed why he'd avoided Park Road. He didn't want to bring up disagreeable memories. She squeezed his waist to show her appreciation.

They alighted in Park Avenue instead of going into the main car park, and Sam pulled out his GPS unit.

"Somewhere around the flowerbeds, Vee." He gestured to the footpath ahead of them.

"Will the scooter be safe here, Sam?" There were more people around than was usual for a Sunday morning, thanks to the sun, and while the good burghers of Solihull might generally be trusted to behave with civility and decorum, it was always possible that some infraction or infringement of the social code had been unwittingly performed by abandoning a German scooter so blatantly in public. Some of the stuffier and more Blimpish Silhillians might take its very presence as incitement.

"It's fine, Vee. Don't worry." Sam was more interested in finding the cache.

They followed the main footpath through the park, Ivy offering a hello on occasion to the other promenaders, Sam rarely paying them any heed, observing the changes in the co-ordinates on his unit and looking up only when attempting to compare their location with his suspicions concerning the cache's whereabouts. After a hundred and fifty yards or so, before reaching the boundary by the Sixth Form College, they veered onto the grass, in the direction of the playing fields.

As they crossed towards the flowerbeds, Ivy saw, in the distance, a flock of flamingos standing in the pond across the park. From among them, a single, rogue female took flight, either freaked by a sudden noise or exercising her independence.

"Sylvia," said Ivy softly, but Sam wasn't on hand to hear.

"Over here, Vee."

She realized he'd wandered off. He was at the edge of an oval bed of tulips, lined with Little Dorrit, with an inner band of purple pansies separating the two. As she joined him, he motioned with his head.

"Somewhere hereabouts."

"Are you serious?"

"Can't argue with the technology, Vee."

She looked around nervously.

"Surely it's irresponsible to hide a cache in the flowerbeds. We can't go trampling all over. Someone'll call the parkie on us."

"Maybe it's around the edge somewhere," Sam said. "Or buried, perhaps. The Hint said 'Don't tiptoe.' Like, 'Don't tiptoe through the tulips'."

"Mmm." She was unconvinced. "It might mean 'Don't tiptoe: Stomp!' See if there are any footprints in the soil. I don't want to start digging up the flowers."

"Good thinking, Vee."

Together they limned the edge of the bed, peering for signs of disturbance in the earth, but after completing the circumference, they remained nonplussed.

"Do you think the Hint is a size reference, Sam? Not tulips at all, but Tiny Tim. Is it a reference to the Little Dorrit?"

"Maybe. You could be right." He had his doubts but preferred to postpone the alternative option of wading into the flowers. "Take a closer look at them. There might be something awry."

Sure enough, there was. Working their way round either side of the flowerbed, Sam anti-clockwise, Ivy clockwise, they met up at the other side. Their eyes met momentarily before simultaneously spotting the imitation flower at their feet.

"Of course, it's a fake Little Dorrit," said Ivy.

"Must be a plant," Sam joked.

"Well, then," she said, responding with an equally bad pun, "Let's get to the root of the matter."

She knelt down and, with a little effort, pulled it from the soil. Hidden beneath, attached to a plastic base, was a round tin canister. A press-stud held down the lid; Sam released it and peered inside before emptying the contents out.

A beermat, a model cowboy on horseback, a small box of candles for a birthday cake, a lock and key for luggage, and … where was the token?

"Is that the lot?" Ivy said, her disappointment shared but not expressed by Sam, who was holding the can over his head and squinting inside.

"Hold on. There's something stuck in the bottom." He reached in with his hand and pulled out what looked like a red handkerchief.

"Maybe it's wrapped in this." He unfurled it. "Yup. Here it is."

Ivy wasn't looking at the token. Had she done so, she would have seen the same M pattern shared by the other tokens and, on the obverse side, the ancient Christian symbol for a fish, except with a line crossed through it. A symbol that clearly meant … no fish.

She wasn't looking at it because her attention was focused on the red silk handkerchief. Only it wasn't a handkerchief at all. It was a cravat.

"What the hell's going on, Sam? That's Ned's cravat."

"Ned? Are yow sure?"

"Absolutely. Look. It's even got his bloody initials on."

Sam couldn't recall the last time he'd heard Ivy swear. This was serious.

"Surely it's not Ned who's been planting the caches. What do yow think he's up to?"

"I don't know, Sam, I don't know." Ivy's jaw clenched. "But we're going to find out. He's only up the road. They have a service in the Tabernacle every Sunday morning. I think we should pay him a visit, don't you?"

Her agitation verged on anger, something she'd never truly experienced. She'd encountered irritation before, but never this kind of iridescent rage. She'd never had the confidence, the self-belief, to feel justified in getting angry. Yet now she was fuming. Quietly fuming, admittedly, but it still counted.

"Have yow got the other tokens with you?"

"I always have them, Sam. In my purse. I carry them around for luck."

"Well then, I'm right behind yow, Ivy. Let's give the bastard a call."

Chapter Twenty-nine

And slew they the monster of Al-Khad-Rins-r, but many of their own did fall thereunto also. Strong was the monster on all the maidens they had fed it. Bloody idiots.

Grampus 8:19

They decided to leave the Durköpp where it was. Park Road was twenty minutes away, but Ivy marched the entire distance in indignation. Sam did his best to keep up and match her intensity.

She had been right. There was a service on. The main auditorium doors were wide open and she could see as she approached that there were a good two hundred worshippers within, their backs to her, rapt in awe at the demonstration of charismatic leadership being provided by George Hartfield, up on the stage, directly ahead of her, straight down the aisle. Flanking him, she noticed, were Ned and his mother, the former nodding sagely as his father read to the congregation from the documents laid out before him on the pulpit of his Segway.

"Thus did they cut off his hand and slap him with it in his own face; for he belonged to a tribe different from their own," he boomed. "And when they had castrated him, they laid him down and urinated on his body and his wounds."

Ivy did not notice the consternation she was causing, nor did she recognize the faces of those who followed her passage, faces she'd seen at the party, at the Donkey Derby. There was Sylvia, there was the mayor and his wife, there was Miss Walsall 1998. She just strode straight down the aisle, whipping the tokens from her purse as she neared the stage.

"Ned Hartfield! Tell me the meaning of this! Tell me what your game is! Tell these people what you are!"

The response was the rumbling and mumbling of confused churchgoers. One or two rose from their seats for a better view of this interloper, to see what the commotion was, but none had the courage to intervene, to prevent her from reaching the foot of the stage, Sam following closely behind.

"Tell me the meaning of these!" she demanded and tossed the four tokens across the floor of the stage at his feet.

Almost as one, the congregation stood to see what she had thrown. Calmly, almost serenely, Ned, who had remained poised since her entrance, shifted forward from his seat and gathered together the tokens, crouching as he did so, before reaching to his full height. Addressing the throng at the top of his voice, he held up the tokens for all to see.

"Behold! She bears the four augurs of Mogadon!"

A gust blew through the crowd like the breath of God.

"It is the Prophet," they said as one. "The scripture is fulfilled." The scraping of wood on wood caused Sam and Ivy to spin round, as the entire congregation fell to their knees and bowed their heads in Ivy's direction. She looked at Sam in total confusion. He couldn't help her. She'd been well and truly set up. Set up, it seemed, for worship.

And then it dawned on her. The text George Hartfield had recited. She'd *thought* it sounded familiar.

"That's my research you're reading. That isn't scripture. It's accounts of murder."

"It is the Transcendental Gospel," said Hartfield triumphantly. "The Good Lord promised us, his chosen ones, a new covenant and a prophet who would bring it in ignorance. She who bore the four augurs of Mogadon. Promised in the Book of Obfuscation."

"All praise the exegesis of the ferblet," came the muffled response from the still-bowed congregation.

"You can't use my descriptions of genocide and torture as the basis for a new religion. I won't let you."

She looked for steps up to the stage. There didn't seem to be any.

"Why not? It's so pure. So perfect. All the old gospels contradict one another, leave themselves open to misinterpretation. The new gospel is as one: consistent, coherent, all-encompassing."

"It's a prescription for evil is what it is. You can't base a religion on that."

Hartfield addressed the congregation once more.

"Again the scripture is fulfilled. 'For the Prophet, she who has knowledge but no wisdom, will renounce the covenant before you, my people. Therein lies the proof of its true provenance: I, the Lord, thy God'."

"Prophylactics 24:7," they replied, one or two sneaking a peek to see what was happening.

What was happening was that Ivy and Sam had scampered to the side of the stage and were trying to climb up, in the absence of steps, while Ned did everything he could to keep them down.

"Give me back my research, Ned. You can't use it like this."

"It's the property of the Hartfield Foundation," he said smugly. "It isn't yours at all. You've been paid for the work. I'd have thought you'd be happy. Don't you want to be worshipped? Isn't that what every woman wants?"

"You bastard."

It was at that moment that the cavalry appeared. Okay, not the cavalry: the deus ex machina. Me and Jack. And not actually the deus ex machina. More like the diabolus.

"Hold it right there, Hartfield!" Jack said, to announce our arrival. "You're not getting away with it this time."

"Pance!" shouted Hartfield.

"The Beast!" cried the congregation, recoiling in horror, cowering, retreating from us along the pews for all their worth as we ambled towards the stage. Their declaration, I should point out, had been directed at Jack, not me. What they clearly should have said was, "The Beast! ... and his dog!"

Ivy and Sam looked confused but pleased to see us, imagining we could provide answers and support. But Jack was annoyed.

"You were supposed to tell me if you found the fourth token," he said.

"I know, Mr. Pance. I'm sorry," said Ivy. "But it seems the Hartfields' scriptures have preordained my actions right from the start of this book."

"They're not scriptures," said Jack, amused at her continued innocence. "Hartfield and I wrote those texts back in the eighties. Why don't you tell everybody, George?"

"Blasphemer!" shouted Ned, trying to arouse the congregation but probably protesting too much. "See how the Beast tries to corrupt you with his lies!"

"Tell them, George." Jack figured that Ivy, for one, deserved an explanation. "Tell them about the game we invented. Super fun, wasn't it?"

"Game?" said Sam, more interested than he should have been in this sudden revelation.

"Yes, Sam. A board game. Messiah, we called it. Those tokens you showed me, the ass, the blind man, they were counters from our game, from the pre-production version." He smiled with a touching contempt for his younger self. "Oh, we were very clever, George and I ... weren't we, George? We even wrote our own Bible to provide a backstory for the game."

"How did yow play it?" This wasn't the time or place for a detailed explanation of the rules, and Ivy gave Sam a sharp elbow the moment he had the question out.

"It was simple enough." Jack said. "The backstory provided a set of prophecies foretelling the coming of a messiah, who would bring a new gospel to the world, and then all the players would have to compete to be the Chosen One."

Ned had jumped down from the stage, frustrated that heads that had long been bowed were being raised, that members of the congregation were listening to Jack and having the veil lifted from their eyes. He squared up to Jack. He was about to forcibly eject an old man from a place of worship, the sort of action likely to generate negative publicity for any religion.

"I never heard of this game," said Ivy.

"You won't have," Jack explained. "I thought better of it, and when George said we should go ahead and market it, I told him he was being daft. We'll look like pontificating dicks, I said, just like those we were condemning. I'll have nothing whatever to do with it. And I was right, of course, he knew that. So instead, he decided he'd start a religion of his own, using the texts we'd written. Despicable, but there was nothing I could do to stop him. He was conning people blind, but they didn't want to hear my side of the story. I didn't offer salvation. All I had to offer was truth."

"OUT!" snarled Ned, taking Mad Jack by the shoulders.

"Begone!" pronounced Hartfield from the security of the stage.

"Get your hands off him," said Ivy to Ned, grabbing his wrist with her hand.

"Get off me!" Ned said and swung out with his arm, catching Ivy's temple with the back of his hand and knocking the Prophet to the floor.

"Oooohh!" went the congregation. That wasn't in the scripture.

I barked.

Sam's punch came out of nowhere. Even he couldn't explain where the energy came from, the venom, but it connected with Ned's jaw at 90 degrees, sending him sprawling among the congregants, scattering them like nine pins, knocking Sylvia's bright green wig clean off her bald head.

"Rocky 3:16," said Sam angrily. "And he did smite the bastard round the head whereuntil he knewest not his own name nor knewest he the name of his kin."

He squatted down next to Ivy, who was still prone and holding her forehead. He put his hand tenderly to her cheek.

"Vee. Are yow okay?"

She nodded.

"Let's get out of here, Sam."

He helped her to her feet, brushed her down, and left, Jack and I in their wake. All very dignified, all very proud. Happy? No. But then happiness isn't everything.

Lying prone among his fellow worshippers, Ned had a moment to reflect that things hadn't turned out that badly, after all. Ivy and Sam had seemed satisfied with an explanation and the opportunity to take a swing at him, and even though his testicles still ached, he and his father had managed to finally get their gospel, as well as a prophet who'd renounced it. What could have been better?

He touched his lip with his tongue and tasted blood where his own tooth had cut it. Reaching into the pocket of his blazer, he pulled out a monogrammed red cravat and wiped the blood away.

Chapter Thirty

Crawl not before those that contemn thee, nor before those that contemneth thee not. Flatter not those who praise thee, nor those who praise thee not. Attend only to those who care. To them address thyself.
Sossages 2 & 6

"From the logic that those creatures most able to adapt to their environment are best able to survive, it follows that those creatures that are most flexible, most capable of adapting to a variety of conditions, will more readily survive changes in the environment. Creatures adapted very specifically to a particular environment are in trouble should that environment change; those able to adapt will perpetuate themselves and their species."

To Ivy, having become the founder of a religion based on man's inhumanity to man, this seemed scant consolation, but she also knew that this was how things were done in Nana's house. She'd had enough time to acclimatize to the conditions, to adapt to the environment, and if she was going to move in there, then she had to exhibit some of this flexibility that Sam was talking about. Much as she'd loved living in Broad Oaks Road, the environment there had become arid, incapable of sustaining her, and she didn't want to see Maggie and Siobhan's friendship break up—Maggie had offered to move out once she understood what had happened with Ned, but Ivy wouldn't hear of it. Events had taken an unfortunate turn, but it was time for Ivy to move on anyway. New home, new job, new ... no, not a new life, not yet, but the kind of life she needed to live right now.

"Naturally," Sam continued, Nana and Caroline listening intently, Nana nodding here and there where his argument met with her approval or where she was ahead of him and knew where he was going, "the opposable thumb has given us a further advantage insofar as we are able to modify the environment itself, making it more hospitable, more habitable, and with the flexibility that has necessarily evolved in human nature has come the very real characteristic of choice, for in any situation, human flexibility is such that we have a number of options available. Given that not every situation is life-threatening, under which circumstances we do not in any case have any choice, we are presented with what, for want of a better term, we like to call free will—the capacity to choose between alternatives."

It was like a tribal gathering, a camp-fire meeting to determine the communal worldview. Ivy had always been allowed in on the Saturday night get-togethers, when nothing more serious than a board game had challenged her and nothing stronger than homemade wine passed her lips. Never before had she witnessed the Sunday night gathering, when, instead of religious teaching, Nana required them to review what they'd learned from life during the previous week. Ironically, Ivy reflected, it was like being initiated into the inner circle of a religious cult.

"Are you saying, Sam, that I shouldn't feel responsible for the decisions other people make to join the Transcendental Gospel Crusade, even though I've provided them with a gospel of brutality?"

She'd interrupted his flow of thought. For a moment, he looked annoyed, then remembered he had to indulge the neophyte.

"That's a valid point, Vee, but it isn't where I was going. I was about to make the observation that the essence of such an ethic, one promulgated by your gospel, is unsustainable. A species in which every individual behaves selfishly will not survive. Competition within a species weakens both the losers and the winners. Either both are wounded and become easier prey for outside predators, or the victor enslaves the conquered, in which case the master becomes a parasite, its energy devoted to sustaining its own rule within the species, and the slave becomes a drone, ground down by work. We should revise the old saw to say, 'that which does not kill me makes me weaker'."

"Except for vaccinations," said Nana facetiously.

"Ahr, Nana, but vaccinations are an example of co-operation within our species to avoid an external threat. In other words," he turned back to face Ivy, his intended audience, "competition between humans is a relatively recent phenomenon. Aggression has always been present, of course, but directed against external threats. It was only where resources were scarce that competition could have arisen. Yet Nature in general is fecund, abundant in riches."

"That was Nietzsche's objection to Darwin, wasn't it?" said Caroline, trying to impress Nana by getting the observation in before Sam did.

"Ahr. That's right. Kropotkin too, I think. The world is full of riches, yet we have extended a way of behaving that is appropriate to scarcity—the desert—to conditions of plenty. Scarcity, such as it is, is artificially created to ensure divisions among the drones."

Bloody hell, thought Ivy, shifting in her chair. This is hard going. I don't know if I'll be able to keep up with this lot.

Then, before she knew it, Sam was next to her and had taken her hand in his.

"People are capable of doing really bad things to one another, Vee, but really good things, too. All yow've done till now is make a record of all the bad things. Maybe, to put things right, all yow need to do is make a record of all the good things people do. Balance the books, as it were." He started to stroke the back of her hand. She let him. "I'll help yow out if yow like. I think yow'll find it'll be quite a substantial tome. Every single day there are billions of acts of generosity, of good deeds, of cooperation. Just because they're not on the news ... well, the job of the news is to report extraordinary events, and if extraordinary events are bad, presumably the ordinary things, the things not worth mentioning because they're so commonplace, are good."

She was searching his face for the old Sam, the sarcastic Sam, the vulgar Sam. She was sure he was in there somewhere, about to come out with a joke about piles, but another Sam had risen to the surface. Gentle Sam, considerate Sam, sympathetic Sam.

"There are billions of kisses every day, Vee," he said, and raised her hand to his lips. Well, that was a bit embarrassing. "Why don't yow tell people about all the kisses?"

This was as intimate as Sam was to get that night, much to Ivy's relief, and the conversation moved on to more arcane and technical issues that needn't concern us right now. There are more pressing matters to discuss.

For one thing, I'm sure you want to know whether or not Ivy was the Chosen One. Let's look at the evidence: The virus that shut down the hospitals and health services across the country was clearly planted by the Hartfields as part of their efforts to generate a series of evil miracles around the life of the Prophet, as was the death of poor Reg Carter under the Number 17 bus when Ivy's pager went off. Someone else must have been watching her, besides Jack and me. The Donkey Derby, of course, was fixed, just to have Ivy ride through the crowds on the back of an ass.

The letter to the papers that Ivy wrote about the evils of alcohol was her own doing, but it suited the Hartfields' purposes perfectly for her to succeed, to transform wine into water, and Ned did everything he could to persuade the Vintners' Association of the merits of Ivy's case. Fortunately—for all of you, I think—he was unsuccessful. You can still have the odd drink when you want, but the blight of alcohol-related violence is something you people have *got* to sort out.

Then there was the incorrect advice that Ivy gave to the guide of the Japanese tourists, sending them somewhere to eat where there was no food. Not quite the Starving of the Five Thousand, just eighty-nine Japanese ELO fans, and this time round Jack was there to put things right. Was it pure coincidence that the coaches had taken the wrong turn-off on the M42 and ended up in Earlswood instead at the Birmingham Arena? Or might it have had something to do with the manifold the drivers had been faxed at the last minute after a phone call from someone claiming to be a temp in head office but who quite conceivably could have been an impostor who occasionally resembled a flamingo?

And what about Ned's cravat? Whose cravat was it wrapped around that last counter if not Ned's? And *had* he been planting the augurs of Mogadon or not?

I can't say for sure who was planting the caches, but the emails Sam received about new caches were not mailshots sent to a group and the website's settings were restricted so that only Sam could see it. Therefore, whoever was planting the caches wanted to make sure Sam was the FTF. Draw your own conclusions. As for the cravat, well, a man can have more than one cravat, can't he? Even identical ones. Some men are like that. They like their routine. Their rituals.

So, was Ivy the Chosen One? In my humble opinion, no. But she was lucky to get away with it. Circumstantial evidence would have pointed in her direction had it not been for Jack exposing the Hartfields. Which only goes to show how small a number of misunderstood, misinterpreted, or deliberately manufactured events are required to establish an undeserved reputation, doesn't it? It could happen to anyone.

You'll want to know what happened to the Hartfields, no doubt. Well, it's in the nature of these stories, of course, that they thrived. Their new religion prospered. It didn't matter to the congregation that their holy texts were based on a board game; after all, hadn't the texts still managed to predict the coming of the Prophet and her renunciation of the new covenant? Truly, that was miraculous, was it not?

Jack and I are still doing our best to campaign against them, and sometimes we have minor triumphs, but this is the real world, and in the real world, bad people can prosper just like the good. Indeed, bad people can prosper *because of* the good. It's like Sam just finished telling Ivy: the bad people are parasites, free-riders, taking advantage of our sociability and willingness to trust. It's just fortunate—or an evolutionary necessity, if you believe Sam—that there are more good people than bad.

And what about Sam and Ivy? You want to know whether they got it together, right? Okay. I'll tell you. No, they didn't. Not right away. Sam was still too much like a brother to Ivy, and he'd only had a short amount of time to practice his newly acquired skills in seduction and sexual technique, mostly on himself. In the mirror. That can't have been easy for him. Besides, they had the book to work on first, and Ivy had to do that in her spare time: She started a new job as a librarian in Shirley, which suited her down to the ground. In the evenings, although she was tired, she sat down with Sam and they worked their way through history, compiling examples of cooperation and genuinely philanthropic behaviour for Ivy's new book. She called it *The Book of Kindnesses*. Sam liked that. And just as she had when she compiled her lists of brutalities, she arranged her lists of kindnesses in order of familiarity: The first chapter began with a list of all the kindnesses she had been shown by Nana, and Caroline, and Sam.

When the book was complete, they tried to get it published—you should look for it in the shops—and the free time Ivy then had available was taken up by a new obsession. Sam finally had the opportunity to put into practice everything he learned from Nana. It was awkward, at first, and it was awkward at second, too, and there was a lot of laughing involved in the early experiments, but after a while, and after taking some instruction from Ivy that his Nana could never have given him, Sam managed to get things right; he learned to shower her with whispers, to cascade her with kisses, to touch her with his words and with his fingers, and with his tongue. And one day, one day when they weren't expecting it, but from that one day, nearly every day, to Ivy's delight and elation, they found that their bodies could sing.

THE END

Acknowledgements

The beyond-talented Jon Langford won the 2015 Lord of the Book Covers award for his cover design of *Breakfast at Cannibal Joe's*. I would have been a fool not to ask him to provide the artwork, in his own inimitable style, for Ivy. He really came up with the goods. Thank you so much, Jon. Again. Effusive, heartfelt, and endless gratitude is also owed to my brilliant beta-readers, Stephanie Ní Thiarnaigh and Estelle Birdy, who provided me with generous amounts of honest, sharp, and super-smart feedback. Basil Henrick's excellent geocaching advice was also immensely helpful, providing me with all the essential details and pro-tips that I hope lend a greater air of authenticity to at least one aspect of Ivy's Grail Quest. Cheers, Basil. My brother Martin proved once again to be a reliable touchstone and source of inspiration. You're a star, Mart. Clare Daly at the *TBR Pile* and Darragh Geraghty at the *Bloomfield Review* gave permission for the inclusion of their reviews of *Breakfast at Cannibal Joe's*. Many thanks to them and to Carlton, Lisa, and William for their kind and complimentary words, with a special mention to Niamh, my favourite romcom novelist, who provided the comment you see on the cover. I am also grateful to the staff of Solihull Borough Council's Parks and Open Spaces Department, who provided me with a refresher course in the flora and fauna of Palmers Rough, where I (mis)spent many happy childhood hours chasing after footballs, skidding my bike through puddles, falling out of trees, grazing my knees and elbows, and showing girls mine in exchange for seeing theirs. Belated thanks too to those girls. You know who you are.